MEETING MOLLY

With £4.07 in her bank account, the rent due, and her party-planning business foundering, Sarah-Louise is forced to look for a job. Spotting one in the paper, she makes the call and soon meets Olly, who is looking after his sister's dog Molly for six months and needs someone to walk her. Sarah-Louise takes a fancy to him — but after dealing with an AWOL Molly, a jealous flatmate and a worrying attack on Olly, could the two of them possibly have a future together?

CHRISSIE LOVEDAY

MEETING MOLLY

Complete and Unabridged

LINFORD
Leicester

First published in Great Britain in 2018

First Linford Edition
published 2019

A catalogue record for this book is available
from the British Library.

ISBN 978–1–4448–4258–6

Published by
F. A. Thorpe (Publishing)
Anstey, Leicestershire

Set by Words & Graphics Ltd.
Anstey, Leicestershire
Printed and bound in Great Britain by
T. J. International Ltd., Padstow, Cornwall

This book is printed on acid-free paper

Desperate Measures

Sarah-Louise sat contemplating. She kept looking at the phone, willing it to ring. Her share of the rent was due at the end of the week and she had £4.07 in her bank account.

Her purse contained 59 pence and that was only half of what she owed her friend and flatmate Jeannie for the teabags she had bought the previous day. Life was dire. She sighed again. What was she supposed to do?

At five o'clock, her friend came home. She dumped her bags and moaned.

'Our wretched Head. She cleared off at three o'clock for the third day running. No explanation, nothing. Just went off in her flashy car to who knows where? I don't know how she keeps her job. She's useless and an absolute pain in the rear. Any tea going?'

'I'll put the kettle on. I say, Jeannie, can we talk?'

'That sounds serious. Only after I'm sitting with a steaming mug of tea in my hand. After the day I've had, I don't want to hear anything unpleasant at all.'

Sarah-Louise went into the kitchen and put the kettle on. Oh dear, she was thinking. It does not sound good. Poor Jeannie really was having a bad time. But at least she had a job, which was more than she had.

Her friend was always supporting her financially but Sarah-Louise usually managed to pay her back eventually. She poured boiling water on a teabag and fished it out and dumped it in her own mug.

At least she couldn't be accused of being wasteful. She even drank hers black to make sure the milk lasted out.

'There you are,' she said, handing over the tea.

'Bless you, love. Thanks. Now, what's the problem?'

'The usual. No work, no money. The rent is due and I've got nothing in the bank. Well, unless you count four pounds and seven pence.'

'Heavens. Is that really all you've got?' Jeannie was incredulous. 'How on earth can you let things get so low?'

'I can't demand people have parties for their children. What am I supposed to do? Go out into the streets and say, 'Hey, look at me. I can do kiddies' parties. Why don't you book me right away?''

'It really isn't working, is it?'

Sarah-Louise looked down.

'Nope. It used to be good and I was always a hit. Somehow, kids today don't really go for it in the same way. Trouble is, I'm no good at anything else.

'Look at the time I took that job in the boutique in the high street. One week and I was told, 'We'll have to let you go.' In other words, I was useless and got fired.'

'You shouldn't have been so outspoken to your customers. Nobody likes to

3

be told something makes them look like a pork pie.'

Jeannie began to giggle at the memory. Eventually Sarah-Louise joined in.

'OK, shop assistant is out. You could always go to a supermarket. Contact with customers is a bit more remote there.'

'I did try that once.'

'And?'

'I told a customer their trolley was full of dreadful food that would make their family as fat as she was. She really was huge, I'm not kidding. She complained to the manager and I was out. Don't people like to learn about their diets?'

'Possibly they do. But not like that. Honestly, your tongue runs away, with itself.'

'Must be my background. I was always taught to say what I was thinking.'

'You never even finished your drama school, did you?'

'Course not. They were all so boring.

All that breathing and pretending to be a tree. Not sure what that had to do with acting. 'Project,' they kept on saying. I stuck it for over a year and then decided it was not for me. I'd love a job on television. I can just see me acting with some gorgeous male.'

'Oh, for heavens sake S-L . . . be realistic. You have to find a proper job. Earn some serious money.'

'Television is pretty serious.'

'You'd never get on television. Why not try demonstrating something? A household product everyone will want to buy?'

'Actually, I have tried that too. It was a sort of vacuum cleaner affair. I had to sprinkle dust over a piece of carpet and prove how good it was at cleaning up.'

'So? What went wrong with that?'

'The bag of dust, actually. I tried tipping a bit out and the whole lot fell out. Everyone started sneezing, including me. I tried to pick it up with the cleaner but it jammed and wouldn't pick up anything.

'I stood there with a cleaner in my hand and sneezing and red-eyed for about half an hour. People were taking pictures of me with their phones. Talk about embarrassing.'

'Strikes me you're a walking disaster area.'

'When it comes to work, I suppose I am. Perhaps your head teacher will resign and I can get her job. Couldn't cause much chaos in a school, could I?'

'Not sure about that. How about being a barmaid? No, forget that one. Far too many problems there.' Sarah-Louise was drawing breath and starting to tell her of her barmaid experience. 'No more, please. It's too depressing.'

'So, basically, can you lend me some dosh till I've solved my current problem? I'm really sorry to have to ask but you know how it is.'

'I suppose so. But we do have to sort you out somehow. Let's make a list of what you can do well.'

'Pretty short list. I can drive fairly well. Not that I've been driving much lately. My car has got a SORN on it at present. Can't afford to keep it on the road. I can use a computer.'

'Then maybe that's something you could do. People are always asking for computer literate people.'

'There's a difference between being able to use it and actually doing anything clever with it.'

'OK. Cancel computer operative. You can cook reasonably well. A kitchen job, perhaps?' Jeannie peered at her friend, waiting for her to tell some story about burning a kitchen down or something. Nothing came. 'Well? Could you be a cook somewhere?'

'I could do outside catering. You know, make lavish dinner parties for wealthy people. I have done that in the past.'

'Be realistic, for goodness' sake. You haven't had any bookings for ages. You need to get some money quickly. I can only support you for so long and you will have to pay me back.'

'OK. I'll look in the paper right away.

Can you lend something to go and buy one?'

'Oh, for goodness' sake! I picked one up on my way home. Did you manage to get anything in for supper?' Sarah-Louise shook her head. 'Might have known. Fortunately, I picked up some mince in case you hadn't. I suppose you didn't have time.' Her friend hung her head, feeling ashamed.

'I'll cook anyway. Least I can do.'

'You're not kidding. I've got some marking to do. I'll leave you to it. Make whatever you like.' Jeannie settled down with a pile of papers and started to get immersed in the essays.

Sarah-Louise picked up the packet of mince and wondered what to do with it. She was severely limited by the absence of anything to put with it. No tomatoes, canned or otherwise, and no rice. There were a few tatty-looking potatoes and half an onion in the fridge. Shepherd's pie, she murmured to herself. Or something vaguely resembling that.

She remembered the paper and

looking for a job. She very much doubted anyone would be asking for someone to organise their child's party. That was really what she did best.

Sarah-Louise began to fry the mince with the chopped onion, dreaming of her ideal job. A handsome bloke, hopefully separated from his wife . . . no, preferably widowed and left with a small girl, who wants to invite her friends from school or nursery. She would dress up in her princess outfit, complete with wand to provide magic.

She stirred the mince and wondered what she could add to make it seem like a proper meal.

'Could do with a magic wand for this meal,' she murmured.

'What did you say? Sorry. Just heard you muttering but couldn't make out what you said.'

'Nothing. Just talking to myself. Could I look at the paper, please? Didn't want to disturb you.'

'Help yourself. It's in my bag. Oh, I

bought a bottle of wine too, to cheer us up.'

'You're an amazing person, Jeannie. Thank you very much. Should I pour some for you?'

'In a while. How's supper coming on?'

'Perfect. You'll love it.' She crossed her fingers behind her back and took the evening paper out of Jeannie's bag. She turned to the situations vacant page. Quickly, she scanned the various options. There seemed to be nothing she was capable of doing.

'Do you think I could be a wedding planner?' she asked.

'No. You're not organised enough for that.'

'Why not? I can be organised with the best of them.'

'What on earth do you know about weddings?'

'Bride and groom. Big fluffy dress. White chairs for people to sit on. Possibly with bows on. Lots of hats. Must have lots of hats.'

'Exactly. Like I said, what do you know about weddings?'

'OK. Probably not enough. That big computer company needs a cleaner. That's about my sort of job.'

'You, a cleaner? I don't think so, love. Your room is a mess, for a start.'

'That's just me being creative with the space. OK. Scrub the cleaning. Scrub it. Get it?'

'Unless it's important, please leave me in peace for a while. Once this lot is done, I'm all yours. Go and get on with supper.'

Sarah-Louise went back into the kitchen and peeled the potatoes. The mince was cooked and she turned the heat off. She needed to put some gravy powder in the pan and there wasn't any left. They really did need to do a big shop and stock up.

She found some flour and mixed that with water and put it into the mince. It did look a bit better.

She eyed the bottle of red wine and decided to open it and add a bit to the mince. Better still. Once the potatoes were cooked, she mashed them with a little of the precious remaining milk and put them on top of the mince in a pie dish. This went into the oven to brown off.

She glanced at the paper again. Perhaps she could be a dog walker. Someone wanted a person who loved dogs to walk their pooch.

Didn't pay much but perhaps she could start a dog round and walk several, even at the same time. It would be good for her fitness, too. She had to make up her mind to call the advertiser or should she discuss it with Jeannie? She picked up the phone and dialled the number.

'Hello?' she said as she heard a voice.

'Hello.'

'Regarding your advert in tonight's paper. About someone to walk your dog? Will I do?'

'I'm not sure. What do you know about dogs?'

'Furry. Leg at each corner. Two ears.

You know the sort of thing.' The man at the other end was obviously trying not to laugh.

'I'm not sure you'd be quite right. Thanks for phoning anyway.'

'Please,' she almost squeaked, 'I really need this job. I'm stony broke and the rent is due on Friday. I'll walk the legs off your dog, I promise.'

'Hope you don't. Can you come round this evening? Then we can see if you're suitable and if you get on with my dog.'

'Brilliant. Where do you live?'

'The Berkley side of the park. Wereton Crescent.'

'Sorry? Are you talking of Truro? That's where we live. Or relatively near.'

'No. It's Porthcullion. Perhaps that's a bit too far for you. Thought I'd said that in my advert.'

'Oh, yes. I can see it is. Problem is, I don't have a car. Well, I do, but it's not on the road at the moment. I've got it on a SORN. Can't afford the insurance at the moment. Sorry, you don't want to hear all this.'

'Carry on chatting if you want to. You've got a nice voice. Pity you don't live a bit closer. I'm sure you'd have been fine.'

'I'm sorry to have bothered you.'

'No bother. I'm sorry, too. It would have been nice to get to know you.'

'Likewise. What do you do?'

'Boringly, I work in an office in Truro.'

'Perhaps you could bring your dog into Truro and I could collect him and walk him. I could always bring him or her back to our place afterwards. Keep him there till you finish work.'

'Now there's an offer I can't refuse. OK, you're on.'

'Wow, that's terrific. Give me your work's address and I'll pick him up tomorrow.'

'He's a her. She's very friendly and I'm sure you'll get on famously.'

Sarah-Louise wrote down the address and at last hung up the phone. At least

Jeannie couldn't complain that she hadn't made an effort. She smelled a slight burning smell invading the kitchen.

'Oh, heavens, the pie!' she squealed. But it was all right. A bit of the meat had boiled on to the baking tray and that was what was causing the smell.

'Ready, Jeannie!' she called. She collected cutlery and plates and took them into the other room. Jeannie was slumped over the table fast asleep. 'Wake up, sleepy head, supper's ready. Jeannie?' She was so deeply asleep Sarah-Louise was scared for a moment. Jeannie opened her eyes.

'What?' she murmured. 'I was dreaming about a gorgeous bloke and now he's gone for ever. Ah, well. Can't win 'em all.'

'I've got a job,' Sarah-Louise announced.

'Really? Doing what?'

'Walking someone's beloved pooch.'

'That's not going to bring in much dosh.'

'Well, no — but it could grow into

15

larger round. Oh yes, there's just one thing. I've promised to collect him . . . her . . . from the chap's office and well, then to bring her back here till he finishes work. He'll collect her from here. Hope that's OK?'

'What sort of dog is it?'

'Oh, I didn't ask. Probably some small fluffy thing I expect. Anyway, I'll get the pie.'

How could she have been so stupid? She hadn't asked what breed it was and not even what did he — she — look like. Still, there surely wouldn't be all that many people with a dog in the car at the same office site, would there?

'Here we have one shepherd's pie,' she said with a smile. She had to admit, it didn't half look good. She served generous portions and poured the wine.

'Well done you. Looks lovely.' Jeannie tucked in hungrily and asked for a second helping. 'Didn't have time for any lunch today so I do feel extra hungry. So, what time do you collect your furry friend?'

'Nine o'clock on the dot. Or rather five minutes before nine.'

'And what's the name of the chap?'

'Er, I'm not sure. John, perhaps?'

'Best of luck. You've agreed to look after a dog whose breed you don't know from a chap whose name you don't know and collecting him from some office tomorrow.'

'I'm sure it will be fine,' Sarah-Louise said somewhat uncertainly.

'Best of luck is all I can say. Have some more wine.'

A Big Challenge

It took Sarah-Louise far longer to walk to the office than she was expecting. It was one minute past nine when she arrived, breathless and having run for the past five minutes. She walked past the row of cars and couldn't see any with a dog in them.

She looked around anxiously and saw someone walking their dog towards her. In fact, it looked more like a small pony. The man came closer and smiled at her.

'Hello,' he said. 'I'm Olly Jones. And this is Molly. You must be . . . ?'

'Sarah-Louise. Pleased to meet you. Hello, Olly and hello, Molly. She's big. Very big.'

'Oh, dear. You didn't ask what sort of dog she is. She's a Newfoundland. Very friendly and rather soppy. She isn't too big for you, is she?'

'No, course not,' she said uncertainly. 'Hello, Molly.' The huge dog wagged its tail and settled down on the pavement.

'Sorry. She does that whenever I stop. Look, I must go in now. I hope you'll be all right with her. Can I call you later on? Just to make sure you're coping.'

'It'll be fine. OK, then. Bye. Say bye to your owner.' Molly ignored what she was saying and lay down ready to go to sleep.

'Bye, then. I'll see you about half past five.'

Sarah-Louise walked back towards their flat and Molly wandered along with her, not wanting to be hurried. She kept stopping and Sarah-Louise gave her a gentle tug on the lead. The dog stopped again and deposited the largest heap of poo she had ever seen.

What was she supposed to do with that? Not being an experienced dog walker she had no bags or anything else she could use.

Molly looked pleased with herself

and walked on as if she had done nothing.

Sarah-Louise looked around. Nobody else was around so she left the incriminating evidence and walked on, praying no-one had seen her. She didn't want to be fined. She walked quickly round the next corner.

For how long should she walk this huge beast, she wondered. It probably needed more exercise than she'd had in several months.

There was a patch of land near their flat. She would take Molly there and perhaps let her off the lead so she could run around, always assuming she could run. She didn't really look the running type.

At last they reached Sarah-Louise's flat. She was so glad it was a ground floor and thus avoided her having to haul this pseudo-pony up a flight of stairs.

If only she had the use of her car, she could take the dog to the beach and let it run round and get thoroughly tired, then it would sleep for the rest of the day.

Mind you, she was thinking, the dog seemed to have settled down fairly quickly as it was. She decided to make some toast as she had left home before breakfast.

Molly raised her head and looked vaguely interested as she put two slices of bread in the toaster.

'This is for me, Molly, do you hear?' The dog wagged a huge tail which thumped on the floor and practically rocked the place. Molly heaved herself up on to her feet and sniffed the air expectantly. 'No, this is mine,' Sarah-Louise repeated. 'I expect you had your breakfast before you left home.'

Molly stood looking at the toaster and waiting, slobbering slightly. Sarah-Louise made some coffee but the dog was still staring at the toaster. Sarah-Louise buttered the toast and Molly almost went into a frenzy. Well, a laid-back Molly sort of frenzy.

Sarah-Louise sat down at the table and started to eat her toast. The dog stared at her until she felt so guilty she almost had to give her the rest. She broke a small piece off and gave it to her. It disappeared so quickly she felt it hadn't touched the sides. She looked at the clock. Nine forty-five. It was going to be a long day.

Sarah-Louise began to wonder what on earth she had taken on. She had been expecting a small fluffy sort of dog or at least the smallest spaniel type but this was completely over the top.

She couldn't even vacuum the place as there seemed to be very little of it left when Molly was lying down. She was afraid she had made a big mistake.

'Come on then, beastie, let's see what's on television.' She went into the other room and switched on the set. She watched 'Homes Under the Hammer' and then something about people moving to the other side of the world. Molly snored through them all.

Perhaps she needs to go out, Sarah-Louise was thinking. Maybe another walk?

'Come on then, Molly. Let's go for walkies. Come on.' The dog raised one eyebrow and settled down to sleep again. Sarah-Louise's phone rang.

'Hello?' she said.

'It's Olly,' came a voice. 'Just wondering how you're getting on?'

'She's fast asleep. I asked her if she's ready to go out but she didn't do more than raise one eyebrow.'

'She doesn't usually go out again, once she's well, done her business.'

'Oh, she did that all right. On the way back here. I'm afraid I didn't have anything to put it in so I just left it.'

'Oh, dear. You were lucky no-one saw you. I must give you a supply of bags . . . assuming you are going to see her again.'

'Well, yes, I suppose so. Haven't got anything else to do with my time.'

'Brilliant. I can't tell you how much this means to me. I was so worried about leaving her in my house all day.'

'What on earth made you choose such a large dog?'

'I didn't choose her. She's my sister's dog. She had to go abroad and well, she asked me to have her. It's only for six months but she was desperate. Of course, I couldn't say no. So I'm lumbered.'

'Six months? That's quite a long time. I'm not sure I can have her here for six months. I mean having her for the occasional day perhaps, but . . . '

'I can quite understand. I'll collect her after work today and pay you then. Thanks for having her anyway. I'll have to think of something else.'

'OK. Thanks. I'll see you later.' They hung up and she sat feeling guilty.

Sarah-Louise reasoned with herself. She could still look for work as a party planner and provider with the dog lying there fast asleep.

She got out her computer and began to scan a few pages. She typed in 'Children's parties' and saw a whole lot of people who wanted to organise them. Most of them were in London, though, which was miles away.

Perhaps she should make a website. A few pictures featuring her dressed as a princess or cowgirl and anything else she could think of, should do the trick. She began to doodle around a few ideas and grew quite enthusiastic. Why had she never thought of this before?

She heard a loud grunt and came back to reality. Molly had risen from the floor and was starting to wander round, as much as any dog of that size could wander round in a small flat.

'Do you want to go out?'

The dog seemed to smile at her as if she had found the very thing she wanted. Sarah-Louise rushed to put on her anorak and grabbed the lead.

'Come on then, big girl. Let's go.'

She led the way through the door and the dog followed.

'Good girl,' she encouraged. 'Come on then. Let's go to the park.' After all, she was thinking, this was what she was being paid for. The dog lumbered after her showing as much enthusiasm for her walk as Sarah-Louise was herself.

Eventually, they reached the park or the closest thing to a park in the area. Molly showed no signs of having needed to go out after all.

They walked round the flower-beds and over the neatly trimmed lawns where they were allowed and eventually left the park and went back to the flat.

She put down a bowl of water but Molly wasn't interested.

Perhaps she was missing her owner, or at least her stand-in owner. Olly would be round later. Maybe she would only have a drink when she saw him.

Come to think of it, Sarah-Louise could also do with a drink. She hadn't had lunch, either, but then, there was nothing in the flat to eat, except more toast.

She would go and do some shopping when she was paid. The shops should still be open, providing Olly wasn't too late.

Olly. He was quite nice-looking in a slightly boring way. He wore glasses which she actually quite liked in a man. It gave him an air of seriousness. Not that she had seen much of him so far, but she had felt sort of drawn to him. He'd been very understanding when she'd said she couldn't look after Molly any more.

She glanced down at the huge dog, who in turn looked up at her. Molly's tail wagged and she moved to put a paw on Sarah-Louise's foot. Oh, bless her, she was obviously a happy dog and, really, she wasn't all that much trouble.

'No,' she said out loud, 'I mustn't be swayed. No sentiment here.'

She glanced at the clock. Four-thirty. Sometimes Jeannie came home around this time but she had mentioned there was a staff meeting of some sort so she would probably be late.

Sarah-Louise hoped Olly would be here before Jeannie came home . . . not that she thought Jeannie would mind but she quite fancied the chance to get to know Olly a little. She might even decide to see Molly again tomorrow.

She'd invite him in when he arrived. Offer him some tea. Oh, no, there wasn't any tea left. Coffee, perhaps. He must surely drink coffee.

She removed her foot from under Molly's paw and went to put the kettle on. There was a knock at the door.

'OK, Molly. Here's your owner come to collect you.' The dog showed no interest whatsoever. Sarah-Louise opened the door and invited Olly into the flat.

'She's lying in the room fast asleep. I couldn't get her to show any interest in your arrival at all.'

'She doesn't really know me very well. She's only been with me since last weekend.'

'Come on in. Can I offer you some coffee?'

'That would be great. Thanks.'

'I would offer tea only we've run out. No biscuits, either. Not very good, are we?'

'Not a problem.'

'Oh and it will have to be black. We've run . . . '

'Out of milk. That's OK. I'm always running out of things. I quite like it black.'

'Thanks. That's nice to hear. So tell me about yourself.'

'Not a lot to tell. I'm twenty-six and work in an office. Did go to uni but left after two years.'

'Oh, dear. You're the same age as me. Or nearly. I'm twenty-seven. Last week, actually. I didn't go to uni at all so you're one up on me.'

'I'm going to be twenty-seven next week. Coincidence, eh?'

'Sorry, I'll make some coffee. Do sit down. Won't be a mo.'

'So, what do you do?'

'Mostly I'm a party planner. Kids' parties. I dress up as a princess or a clown or cowgirl depending on the sort of party they want. Only business has been very slack lately. I suppose it's the recession or something.'

'I suppose people aren't giving their kids parties at the moment. Or not ones that involve a planner. Do you do the food as well?'

'I can do. Most mums like to do that themselves but I do offer it if they want it.' She handed him a mug of coffee.

'Sounds good. How often do you do them?'

'Not often enough. Hence the dog-walking idea. I was planning to get several dogs to walk but well, with Molly . . . '

'Yes, she is pretty large, isn't she?' Sarah-Louise nodded. 'Sorry. This hardly going to make you enough to live on, is it?'

'I doubt it.'

'I can up the price as you've had her all day but not by all that much.'

'As I said on the phone, I don't really think it's going to be viable. I haven't really done anything today. I couldn't go to the shops or do any cleaning. Nothing really.'

'I suppose you weren't expecting a

dog this large, were you?'

'Not really. She isn't exactly keen to walk anywhere. I practically had to drag her along.'

'Oh, she does that with me. I always thought it was because she didn't really like me.'

'Where's your sister gone to?'

'America. It's business trip with her husband. I suppose I could tell her Molly's too much to cope with.' The dog lifted its enormous head and stared at both of them in turn, looking distinctly accusing.

'Obviously you can't do that. It would be unfair to her. Molly, I mean. Molly and Olly. Bit much, isn't it?'

'My sister's idea of a laugh. Anyway, I got lumbered and now I need to find someone else to look after her.'

'You need to make sure whoever you get knows she's a giant. I think that's what threw me this morning.'

'I'm sorry, but I was getting desperate. If I'd put that in the advert, would you have phoned in the first place?'

'Probably not. But then, I'd never have known what a Newfoundland was.'

'I'm sorry you've found it a difficult day. I'll give you a bonus. And start the new search for someone to walk her tomorrow.'

'I suppose I could have her tomorrow, if it would help. You'll never find anyone overnight.'

'Really? Would you? I could always drive round here to leave her for you. It's only a few minutes from my office.'

'That would be great. I must say, it was further to walk to your office than I was expecting.'

They chatted for a further half an hour, both of them feeling they were getting on very well. At last, he stood and said he should get home.

'I need to feed this beast. She must be starving. I'll call at the supermarket to stock up on tins of dog food. Hope she'll be all right if I leave her in the car. She fills the back seat so hope she doesn't cause any damage.'

'She might need to go out before she's left any length of time. You can take her into what passes as the garden. It's only a small square of grass but it'll do the job.'

'OK. That's fine. Thanks. So, if I bring her here about quarter to nine in the morning?'

'Great. My flatmate will have left for school by then. I can take Molly for a walk right away — and I'll certainly take a poo bag this time.'

He laughed and led the slightly unwilling dog out of the door. He put her in the car and waved goodbye. He's nice, Sarah-Louise thought. Really nice. And unattached, too.

She went back inside in a sort of dreamlike state, her imagination running riot. She was even imagining her wedding dress. It would be unconventional. Possibly red. Or purple. No, that colour wouldn't suit her at all.

Sarah-Louise saw the money on the table and remembered she needed to go shopping. She rushed out to their nearest shop and picked up a few things they needed, including a pack of frozen fish she could stick in the oven and cook quickly when Jeannie came home.

She also threw a pack of frozen chips into her basket and then decided they needed some peas. Heavens, would her money stretch to all that? She reached the till and sighed a sigh of relief. She had almost £1 left.

When Sarah-Louise got home again, she noticed Jeannie's car in the car park. Oh dear, she had planned to have the meal underway so her friend wasn't kept waiting. She'd be exhausted no doubt.

'Hi, Jeannie. I'm back. How was your day?'

'Exhausting. The Head rambled on and on. She wants us to spend even more time glued to our desks and then working at home so she can leave early every day. Honestly, if everyone did what she does, the whole place would fall apart. If she had to deal with thirty-two wretched kids like mine, she'd never survive. One of them is completely disruptive and dances on the desk given half a chance.'

'Goodness me. Don't you have an assistant in with you?'

'You're joking. I get about two hours a day of someone coming in to help and she's supposed to assist two of the others. I do use her unashamedly to help with the naughty one but mostly it's down to me. I don't know how much longer I can go on like this.'

'Can't you complain to the Head?'

'I could but it wouldn't do me any good. No doubt I'd get a telling off for not being able to control the kids.'

'Perhaps you need a Party Girl like me. I could come and entertain the rest of the class while you sort out the problem pupil.'

'Oh, yes, I'm sure that would work,' Jeannie replied with heavy sarcasm.

'Anyway, enough of my moans. What sort of day did you have?'

'Interesting.'

'Good. Did you collect the dog? Was it fluffy?'

'She. Molly. Oh, yes. Very fluffy.'

'And did you get on?'

'Well, yes. She turned out to be something like a young pony. She's a Newfoundland.'

'What's that?'

'A giant breed. Honestly, she's lovely but simply huge. Very solidly built. I'll find a picture for you later.'

'That must have been tough. Where did you put her?'

'In here. She half-filled the room.'

'Goodness. Why on earth do people get these large breeds?'

Sarah-Louise told her the whole story about the sister going to America and Olly having to look after Molly.

'Olly? And the dog's named Molly?'

'His sister's sense of humour, apparently.'

'Blimey. I'd possibly kill my sister if she did that to me.'

'What? Call her dog by a similar name to you?'

'No, if she bought a large dog and dumped it on me. Anyway, what's for supper?'

'Fish and chips and peas. I'll go and put it in the oven.'

'Excellent.'

The phone rang and Jeannie answered it.

'It's for you,' she called.

Sarah-Louise came in from the kitchen and took the phone.

'Hi, Sarah-Louise. It's me, Olly. Just thought I didn't say thank you for having me and Molly. Oh — and to check you really will have her again tomorrow.'

'Oh, yes. That's fine. Look forward to it.'

'Really?' he said sounding slightly surprised. 'That's good. As I said, I'll see you at quarter to nine. I enjoyed meeting you, and I . . . erm, I wondered if you'd like to have a drink with me one evening?'

'That would be great. I mean yes, I'd love to.'

'OK. That's good. I'll see you tomorrow. We can fix something then.'

'Great. Thanks again. Bye.' She replaced the phone and smiled again.

'I take it that was the lovely Olly? He sounded rather nice. What's he like?'

'Lovely. Quite tall. Wears glasses. Yes, my sort of man.'

'You always did like men with glasses.'

'Yes, I did. Do. He's asked me out for a drink. That was why he called.'

'And what about Molly? Are you seeing her again?'

'I've agreed to have her again tomorrow. He'd never find anyone else tonight and she couldn't really be left on her own all day.'

The evening passed in a flurry of chatter about Olly and Molly. Jeannie hardly got another word in about her awful day. Sarah-Louise gathered she was not looking forward to the next day nor the rest of the term.

'I'm glad you got on so well today but I really need to get to bed now. I feel totally shattered.' Jeannie did look exhausted.

'Sorry if I've been going on a bit,' Sarah-Louise apologised. 'I didn't mean to but it's so rare for anything nice to happen to me. Maybe he's got a brother and we could go out as a foursome. I'll ask him tomorrow.'

'Sarah-Louise, please shut up. I really don't want to go out with some strange bloke. I can find my own boyfriend, thank you very much. Now, please can I go to bed?'

'Course. Sorry. I'll do the washing up.'

'Thanks. Night.'

'Night, love. See you tomorrow.'

Tomorrow. Another day. What was going to happen tomorrow?

Too Good to Be True

Sleeping seemed a bit remote to Sarah-Louise. She tossed and turned and couldn't get Olly out of her mind. It was so stupid. She'd only just met him and didn't know him at all. In fact all she knew about him was the fact he had a sister, was caring for a giant dog and worked in an office in Truro. Oh yes, and he was quite good looking. And he wore glasses. And drove a nice car.

'Go to sleep, you stupid girl,' she muttered and turned over once again. She fell deeply asleep at this point and woke up to hear Jeannie calling her.

'Come on. Your charge will be here in five minutes and you need to get ready.'

'What? I've been awake half the night. It can't possibly be that time.'

'I'm going to work now. Come on.

Get down here right away or you'll miss him.'

Sarah-Louise looked at her alarm clock and shot out of bed. No time to shower. She flung some clothes on and ran into the kitchen. There was a ring at the doorbell.

'Morning, Olly. Morning, Molly.' The large black dog wagged her tail and stepped towards the door.

'Morning, Sarah-Louise. Here she is in all her glory. I've got some poo bags for you, too. Can't expect you to provide them, can I? I'll collect her as last night if that's OK. She'll need a walk fairly soon.'

'Right. I'll take her then. Nice to see you again,' she added somewhat stupidly, she thought. She closed the door as he drove off.

'Right then, Molly dog. You need a walk, do you? Have I got time for a coffee?' The dog was looking very anxious she thought. 'No? Coffee after the walk, then. Come on, girl.'

It was a beautiful morning, sunny

and without the chill that had been blighting the air recently.

'Nearly spring,' she said to the dog.

'Pardon?' an old man said as he walked past.

'Sorry, I was speaking to the dog.'

'I see. I suppose a dog that size is easy to say things to. You're not exactly far away from its ears, are you? Enjoy your walk.'

'Thanks. And you.' She gave a giggle. Talking to a dog did sound rather silly to other people without one. She almost dragged the dog to the rough ground they had visited yesterday. 'Go on then. Do whatever you need to do.'

Molly stood still and Sarah-Louise could have sworn she gazed at her in contempt.

She dragged the dog round three times but it seemed totally unwilling to do anything. She cursed under her breath and started to walk back to the flat.

As soon as they were on the street, Molly stopped and performed a large poo at the side of the kerb.

Sarah-Louise pulled out one of Olly's poo bags, grimaced as she dealt with it, then looked for a bin. There was one along from where they lived so she and Molly went along the street till they reached it.

She posted the bag into the special box and then dragged Molly back to the flat. Hopefully that would be it for the rest of the day and for ever more. She really didn't want to go through that experience again. How did dog owners manage to cope with that every day?

'Right, Molly dog. Hope you're going to settle down like you did yesterday. I haven't had a shower yet and I'm gagging for a coffee. Coffee first, I think. And toast. Definitely some toast.'

Molly raised her head again and licked her lips. Could she possibly know the word toast? Amazing.

'Toast,' Sarah-Louise said again. Molly's head rose, her tail wagged and she licked her lips again. 'OK, I get the picture.' Sarah-Louise grinned. 'I'll make you a slice of toast, too.'

The dog barked. It was a very loud woof.

Olly phoned again around lunchtime to ask if all was well. Sarah-Louise was so pleased to hear his voice. She was being ridiculous, she knew it.

'Your owner has a very sexy voice,' she told the dog, who barely lifted her head.

When the phone rang again later, Sarah-Louise couldn't help feeling disappointed when it wasn't Olly's voice this time.

'Is that Sarah-Louise?'

'Yes it is. How can I help you?'

'Are you free to do a party tomorrow? I'm desperate and really need someone to take over the whole thing.

'It's my daughter's birthday, her fifth, and she's only invited her whole class to come to a party tomorrow afternoon. Of course I knew nothing about it and I have to work in the morning. Can you help?'

'Of course,' Sarah-Louise replied with a small gulp. 'When you say you want me to do the whole thing, does that include food as well?'

'Oh, yes. I don't have time. Is that a problem?'

'No, of course not. You need to tell me what sort of food they like and anything they're into regarding entertainment.'

'Oh, heavens, I've no idea. Can't I leave it to you?'

'Well, yes, of course. I was wondering whether she'd like a princess theme or circus idea?'

'Oh, goodness me, no. She hates princesses and we don't hold with circuses.'

'Cowboys?' Sarah-Louise asked, racking her brains.

'Perhaps animals. She's crazy about dogs. Do you have a dog you could bring?'

Sarah-Louise glanced down at Molly.

45

How would she be with a whole class of kids? Sarah-Louise doubted whether she'd actually wake up sufficiently.

'Possibly. I can do some magic tricks too. OK, a theme is developing. How many children do you expect?'

'Oh, at least fifteen. Is that a problem?'

'Gosh, it must be a small school. I was expecting about thirty or more.'

'Amelia goes to a private school. The numbers are kept small. I wouldn't send her to a state school!'

Sarah-Louise swallowed hard, doing her best not to make derisory comments. She added at least an extra tenner to her bill.

'Excellent,' the caller went on. 'We'll see you around three tomorrow.'

'Sorry, you haven't told me where you live or given me your name.'

'Goodness, I am sorry. My name is Treswillian and I live in Porthcullion. The Grove. Do you know it?'

'No, but I'm sure I'll find it. I'll possibly come a little before three to get things ready. Do you want to know my terms?'

'Don't bother with that now. I'm sure we shall agree with whatever you ask for. Thank you so much. I look forward to meeting you tomorrow.'

'Thank you for your call,' Sarah-Louise muttered to a hung-up phone. 'Oh, heavens, I've now got to plan and cook a load of food and haven't got any money to buy a thing.'

Molly raised herself from the ground and wagged her tail.

'I suppose you want to go out, do you?' Sarah-Louise clipped on the lead and dragged her towards the door. 'Come on, Molly. Be a good pooch.'

They walked along the road towards the park. Molly stopped to sniff several times while Sarah-Louise was busy thinking.

She hoped Jeannie would lend her the car tomorrow and also hoped that Olly would be willing to bring Molly to the party. It was all the same village, wasn't it?

Unless he was occupied with anything else, it surely wouldn't be too difficult?

If he couldn't bring the dog, perhaps she could call to collect her. Mind you, having the giant dog milling around the children might be a little too much.

And what on earth would she wear? A magician's outfit might be tricky. She did have a cloak somewhere and this worn over black trousers and a black T-shirt would have to do.

'Come on, Molly. I need to make some lists.' She dragged the dog round and walked back towards the flat.

She would have to go shopping after Olly had collected Molly and paid her. She hoped Jeannie was having a good day as she needed several favours, not least the loan of some money.

She was about to have a busy evening, too, making cakes and various other things. Sausages, she thought out of the blue. Pizza. That wouldn't take a lot of preparation. She ought to make some sandwiches, too.

Fifteen kids, she was thinking. That wasn't actually too bad. Paper plates and cups. Oh and something to drink.

By the time she arrived back at the flat, her mind was buzzing. She grabbed a piece of paper and began to write lists.

Food was the first heading. She'd buy white and brown bread and make rainbow sandwiches. She'd better make some small fairy cakes, too. She rattled on through her food list. She really didn't want to have too much to do so would rely on some bought products.

Drinks . . . she would get sugar-free ones as she felt sure Mrs Treswillian would make that choice, too. Perhaps she was making more fuss than usual but it had been a while since she had taken an order for a party. Besides, it was going to be profitable, she had no doubt.

There was a knock at the door. She glanced at her watch. Goodness, it was surely not time for Olly? She opened it and saw him on the doorstep. Her heart gave an involuntary leap.

'Olly? I wasn't expecting you.'

'Oh, sorry. We usually finish half an hour early on a Friday.'

'Come in. I'm up to my eyes in work. Someone has booked a party tomorrow and I have to provide food and entertainment.'

'Goodness. How long have you known about it? You should have told me. I could have left her at home.'

'I've known for about two hours. The mum was desperate. Her little darling had invited her entire class to a party tomorrow without telling her. She got to work in the morning so it's yours truly to the rescue.'

'Good gracious! Do you need any help?'

'I can't afford to pay anyone else. But actually, yes, I do need some help. Could you bring Molly round for the kids to pet? It's in Porthcullion. The Grove. Do you know it?'

'Blimey. The Grove is a huge house near the end of the village. You actually want my massive dog to attend a kids' party?'

'Well, yes. Evidently the child is besotted with animals. She'll love Molly. How could she not?'

'OK — but on your own head be it. I won't take any responsibility for her.'

'That would be wonderful. I've got to do some magic tricks . . . perhaps I could make her appear by magic. I think it could work well. Can I phone you tomorrow with a time?'

'Of course you can. It might be fun. I've never done anything like this before. Couldn't I come earlier and help you get things sorted?'

'You surely wouldn't want to spend your afternoon doing anything like that?'

'What makes you say that? I might enjoy it all.'

'You don't strike me a someone who loves children.'

'You don't know me at all.' He looked quite hurt for a moment. 'I was actually engaged at one time . . . She died, and so did our baby.'

'Oh, my goodness. I'm so sorry. I had no idea.'

'How would you? It was a while ago. But I do love children. You can take that as read.'

'Do you want to talk about it?'

'Nope. It's all in the past. So, how can I help you?'

'Really?' Sarah-Louise said uncertainly. He nodded. 'My first task is to go and buy food,' she said. 'Oh, but I can't do that till Jeannie gets back.'

'OK. I could drive you to the supermarket if that's a problem.'

'Not exactly. I need to borrow some money to pay for it all.'

'I've got money.'

'Oh, I couldn't. I'll pay her back tomorrow when they pay me.'

'Have you got a list?'

'Well, yes. Or nearly. Just a few extras to add to it. But what about Molly?

What will you do with her?'

'She can sit in the back of the car. There's plenty of room for the shopping, too. Shall I put the kettle on while you finish your list? I could really do with a cuppa.'

'OK. Coffee's in the kitchen cupboard above the hob.'

'I'm sure I can cope.' He went off whistling softly.

He was too good to be true, she was thinking. Loved kids. Practical. Could possibly cook as well. Wow. She should snap him up right away.

Get on with your list, she ordered herself. Olly put a cup of coffee beside her and stooped to pet the dog. Her tail wagged very gently. She was really a lovely dog and very little trouble. List, she reminded herself.

'OK,' Sarah-Louise said eventually. 'Think that's everything. Are you sure about this?'

'Quite sure. Finish your coffee and we'll go.'

'I'm not sure how to thank you for all

this. It really is very good of you.'

'Not at all. I'm looking forward to doing it. Tell me, what magic tricks can you do?'

'Oh, just simple stuff. It's all matter of distracting them with what I'm saying and then manoeuvring whatever the trick is. Large cards. Juggling balls. Rings that seem to self lock. The usual sort of stuff. Haven't quite worked out how to make Molly appear as if by magic.'

'How about a large box?'

'A giant box, you mean.'

'Or a sheet, maybe?'

'I was thinking about that. Depends on the room. If there's a door somewhere she could just appear though it. Do you think she'd come to me if I called her?'

'I'm sure she would. She seems to like you.'

'Perhaps we can practise when we get back. Oh, sorry, I'm assuming you'd be willing to come back with me.'

'I'm hardly going to leave you in the

supermarket, now am I?' Olly grinned. 'Course I'll bring you back.'

'I wonder if she'll expect me to do goody bags? You know, something for the kids to take home. Oh and I never asked about the birthday cake. I'd better ring her before we leave. The list possibly just got a whole lot longer.' She dialled the number of the last incoming call.

'Mrs Treswillian? I was just wondering if you want me to provide a birthday cake? And goody bags?'

'Oh! Yes, please. I never gave them a thought.'

'How much do you want me to spend on them?'

'Oh, I don't know. A fiver, perhaps? Will that do?'

'That's quite a lot. I mean that will cost seventy-five pounds alone.'

'Do what you think, then. Make it a reasonable bag, though. You know what these children are like.'

'Very well. I really don't mind. It's your money.'

'Of course. I'm thinking three hundred pounds for the whole thing. Is that about right?'

'I'd think so. It depends on the cost of the food as well. But I'm sure that will be fine. Thank you.' Sarah-Louise put the phone down and gave Olly a big grin. 'Hope you can afford what I'm about to spend. It won't be cheap.'

'No worries. Anything up to a fiver.'

'That will buy one party bag. She wants me to spend a fiver on each one. Still, if the house is as good as it sounds, I suppose she can afford it. Come on then. Let's go.'

With Molly hauled into the back of the car, they set off for the supermarket. It was quite busy as it was Friday evening.

Sarah-Louise took a trolley and made a start. Olly had a small basket and was shopping for himself. She was pleased about that as she was already feeling guilty. Jelly, chocolate biscuits, sausages and pizzas were all in the trolley.

She looked at birthday cakes and

decided on a large chocolate creation with Harry Potter's image on the top. She hoped that would fit in with what was becoming the growing theme.

Party bags next. She had some idea of what five-year-olds would like and knowing the sort of fussy mother the child had, she bought lots of things like small writing pads and pencils, small books, balloons and some small toys. She had actually spent nearly £5 on each bag.

Heavens, her trolley was getting very full and she had lost Olly. Paper cups and plates and a table cloth and she was about done. She went towards the tills and bless him, there was Olly standing patiently waiting.

'Sorry to have taken so long. I'm going to be up half the night packing the party bags and as for cooking, well, let's hope I don't fall asleep too soon. Sorry but hope you don't mind paying for all of this lot.'

'Course not. I'll put it on my card. No worries.'

'I can pay you back tomorrow, I promise.'

'Please don't worry about it. Not a problem.'

'Well I do worry. One day, I shall sort myself out financially. It's just been a rather slow time recently. Right. Let's put this lot through.' When Sarah-Louise saw the total bill, she realised that three hundred pounds was barely going to cover what she had spent.

It was over a hundred pounds for the party bags and birthday cake alone. She wasn't going to make a huge profit out of the day.

'I hope you don't mind but I've bought some food for tonight. I assume Jeannie will be with us, too, so I've got some steaks. And a bottle of wine. We can help you pack up the party bags,' he added as if in mitigation.

'Oh, Olly, that's so kind of you. I hadn't given a meal any thought at all. I really will pay you back tomorrow.'

'No, of course not. This is my treat. I

got some salad too. And some nice bread.'

'You are a star. Thank you so much. I know Jeannie will be delighted. It's the sort of meal we dream about! I only usually buy mince and turn it into something edible.'

'I'd be happy to cook while you sort out your shopping.'

'This just gets better and better. I knew you were my sort of man. Thank you very much.'

They loaded everything into the boot and after taking Molly for a short walk, drove back to the flat where Jeannie was waiting.

'Where ever have you been? It's getting on for seven o'clock.'

'Meet Olly. He's the one carrying loads of shopping. He drove me to the supermarket and he's even bought us a fab dinner.'

'Hi, Olly. What on earth has she got you involved in now?'

'Hello, Jeannie. A children's party tomorrow. We're packing party bags this evening. I hope you don't mind Molly coming in?'

'Can't wait. I haven't met her yet. She's made quite an impact on my friend here.'

'Yes indeed. I'm very grateful to her. Come on, girl,' he called to the dog. She pottered in slowly and slumped down with a deep sigh. 'I've bought her some food, too. Hope that's OK? I need to borrow a bowl for her.'

'Sure. There's one in the cupboard. I'll get it.'

Olly went into the kitchen and started sorting out their dinner and feeding his dog. The two girls unpacked the shopping. Jeannie was very impressed with Sarah-Louise's choices for the party bags.

'How sensible. Much better than loads of sweets and other rubbish you usually get.'

'Yes, well the mother said I was to spend about five pounds on each bag, which left me plenty of leeway. She's also very particular about her little darling having nice friends. Do you know, her entire class is only fifteen strong?'

'Crikey. What I could do if I only fifteen in my class. I've got thirty-two. Nobody realises what hard work that is. No wonder some kids get on so well in this world.'

'I think I might need to make sure Olly's OK in the kitchen.' Sarah-Louise went in and saw the grill pan covered in steak. 'Oh, wow. That looks amazing.'

'How do you both like it cooked?'

'Medium rare for both of us.'

'Excellent. How I eat it myself. Have you got a salad bowl?'

'There's a plastic thing we usually use. Will that do?'

'I'm sure it will. Where are we going to eat? Can you organise the table?'

'I'll move my shopping.'

'It's OK, I've done it,' Jeannie called. 'It's enough of a treat to have a meal cooked for us. You need to hang on to this one, Sarah-Louise.' Sarah-Louise blushed and smiled at Olly.

'Excuse my friend. She has no idea what she's saying.'

'I really don't mind being hung on to. Not by you. Besides, you actually seem to like my sister's dog. That has to be a good start.'

'She's lovely. Just a bit large. But she has a lovely nature and seems to settle wherever she is.'

'Oh, believe me, she doesn't. She obviously feels secure with you. And this flat.'

'Well, thank you. I hope she'll be OK tomorrow when we take her to the party.'

'I think she will. Right. This is now ready. Let's eat.'

The three of them sat at the small table and soon, they were all eating and enjoying themselves.

'This steak is wonderful,' Jeannie said.

Olly smiled and Molly raised her head and wagged her tail.

'Molly approves anyway,' he said. 'Now, if you've both finished, we'd better get sorting stuff for this party. What do you need to cook tonight?'

'I suppose I could cook the sausages and possibly make some fairy cakes.'

'Right — well you crack on with that, I'll wash up and Jeannie can start packing the party bags.'

Soon there was a smell of cakes baking and sausages cooking. Sarah-Louise made jellies with fruit in them and popped them in the fridge.

'Just how are you going to transport it all to the party venue?' Jeannie asked.

'Oh. I was going to ask if I could borrow your car?'

'I'm planning to go shopping tomorrow. We need to stock up on so many things.'

'It's OK, I'll come and collect you,' Olly offered.

'Really? You're being very good to me.'

'I'm hoping to persuade you to look after the dog for a while longer. I haven't had time to sort out anything else for her.'

'Course I will. Out of pure gratitude, if nothing else.'

'Thank you. I'd better go home now. It's pretty late.'

'Thank you so much for all you've done and are planning to do tomorrow.'

'Not a problem. I'm looking forward to it. Come on, then, Molly. Time for bed.'

'Night. See you tomorrow.' Sarah-Louise gave a sigh as he drove away. 'I do like him. Lots. Haven't met anyone like him for ages.'

'He does seem nice. I'm sorry to be using my car tomorrow. You know I'd help if you were really stuck. Besides, it means you get to spend the afternoon with Olly. You should thank me.'

'Oh, I do.'

Party Time

Sarah-Louise was up at the crack of dawn. She rummaged about in her wardrobe for her magician's cloak and found a wand. She also retrieved her collection of magic tricks and put the whole lot into a box which she took into the lounge.

Her sleep had been very mixed and she finally decided to get up and make a start on her preparations.

She had done a cookery course some time ago, with the idea of becoming a chef. At least she had passed her hygiene certificate with flying colours so felt reasonably confident about what she was doing. Heavens, it was only a children's party so what could go wrong?

Sarah-Louise made lots of tiny sandwiches with brown and white bread so they looked striped. Kids usually liked things like that. Her next job was to decorate the cakes, which she did with melted chocolate and icing.

There remained just the pizzas to heat through and she decided to leave them till she arrived at the Grove. Luckily, she had kept lots of empty plastic boxes so she packed everything into them.

Soon there was a heap of things ready to take. A rather sleepy-looking Jeannie came into the kitchen.

'Do you want any help?' she mumbled.

'I think I'm all done. Couldn't really sleep so I got up early and abracadabra, here lies a birthday party ready to go.'

'Well done you. Though you should be getting good at it by now. You've been doing it long enough.'

'I really need to find something else to do, actually. I can't go on like this, living hand to mouth every week. Just not on. At my age, I should be well settled into a career.'

'Maybe. Have you had breakfast?'

'No. Forgot about it. Do you want toast?'

'Please.'

'I'll put some in.'

'Sorry, I should be doing it. You must be tired and you've got a long day ahead.'

'Not a problem. Do you want coffee or tea?'

'Coffee, I think. I need something to wake me up. Looks as though you're well organised. I like the jelly dishes. They don't take up too much room.'

'And they match the rest of the tableware. Paper plates and cups and table cloth. Hope this child likes everything. I could be in for a whole lot more parties if the kids enjoy it all.

'I do feel a bit nervous but I'm sure it will all work out. Just hope the mother got it right. The kid sounds like a typical princess type but Mum said no. Nothing like that.'

'Best of luck then, love. When will Olly arrive? I ought to get dressed before he does come. Me in my nightie might be a bit much for him.'

'Watch it, you! He's mine, don't forget. Or maybe I intend to make him mine, if only for the next week or two.'

Sarah-Louise looked at her lists and did a final check. It looked as if everything was there. She hoped there wouldn't be lots of parents as she hadn't provided anything for them.

Still, usually it was down to the hostess to provide wine or tea or something. Nothing like that had been mentioned, so why should she worry?

She just hoped there wouldn't be more than 15 children or they wouldn't get a party bag.

It was time to go and change. She shot to her room and put on her black top and black trousers. She would also grab an apron as someone was bound to spill something on her otherwise immaculate look.

There was a ring at the doorbell. That must be Olly. She ran across to answer it.

'Hi, Olly. You're nice and early. Thanks so much for doing this.'

'No problem. I've got Molly in the car. I thought I could take her for a walk while you're getting things set up. I'll come back later and be there ready to bring her in.'

'Perfect. Everything should be OK in the boot. It's all covered and packed in boxes so shouldn't be a problem.'

They began taking everything out to his car and fortunately, it did all fit in, except for her box of magic tricks and cloak.

'Perhaps they can go in the back with Molly? She won't touch them, will she?'

'Wouldn't think so. You can keep an eye on her anyway while we drive over there. Right. Got everything?'

'I think so. Everything except what I've forgotten.'

'I can always pop back if necessary.'

'Thanks, love. You really are very kind. You do realise you've known me for much less than a week?'

'A week or a lifetime. Makes no

difference. I really feel as if I've known you for ever.'

'Me too. Strange, isn't it? I don't even know what you do, except you work in an office.'

'I hate to say this but I'm an accountant.'

'Why do you hate to say it?'

'Because most people think of it as something incredibly boring. Makes me seem boring, too.'

'I don't find you boring at all. How silly of you.'

'There you are. I'm silly, too.'

'Do you know where we're going?'

'It's just along here. Not far. On the left.'

Sarah-Louise peered through the window and saw the large house standing back with a sweeping drive surrounded by shrubs. She swallowed hard.

'Wow. Hope I'm going to be up to all this.'

'Course you are. It'll be a doddle. Dear little girl who goes to a posh private school. What could go wrong?'

'You obviously haven't met any little girls who go to private school. Especially ones who invite their whole class home for a party without their mother knowing.'

'OK, you've got me there. Go for it. I'm sure you'll be fine. I'll help you carry everything in and then disappear. I can go back home. It's not far. Can you ring me when you're over the tea thing?'

'Will do. Your number's in my phone. OK. Here goes.'

She got out of his car and went to ring the doorbell. A slightly flustered-looking woman answered it.

'Oh, are you the party person? Good. I've only just got in and trying to tidy the place up is proving tricky. One very excited little girl.'

'I suppose that's to be expected. I'm Sarah-Louise. How do you do?'

'Yes indeed. Hello. Have you got things to bring in? I hope you have.'

'We'll make a start then, if that's all right.'

'Yes . . . yes. Do whatever you need. Amelia, please. Stop shouting. Tidy up your presents please, darling. Looks as if a bomb's hit the place.'

'Don't want to. I want to play with all of my new things.'

'You need to go and change. Put on your new party dress.'

'No. I'm too busy.'

'But darling, your friends will be here soon. Sarah-Louise has come to organise your party.'

'Don't care. Don't like her.' The child stamped her foot and sat down on the ground.

She's one of those sort of kids, Sarah-Louise thought. Great. It was obviously going to be a real fun afternoon. She smiled and gritted her teeth.

'Hi there, Amelia. I'm pleased to meet you. I hope you're going to enjoy seeing all your school friends in your home. I've got lots of ideas about how you're going to enjoy entertaining them.'

'You're stupid,' Amelia announced.

'Really? I didn't know that. I'd better go away then and find someone else to enjoy all the lovely food I've got in the car.'

'What have you got?'

'Loads of things.'

'All right. You can bring them in. I'll see if I like them.'

Sarah-Louise went out to the car and started bringing in the boxes. Olly helped with carrying, smiling at Mrs Treswillian and trying not to tread on Amelia who was now bouncing round the hall like a demented rocket.

'What's your name?' she demanded.

'Oliver — only my friends call me Olly.'

'Am I your friend?' she asked.

'Could be.'

'What do I have to do to be your friend?' He pulled a face as if he was thinking deeply.

'Be a good girl for your mummy.'

'Nah. Not worth it.' She continued to dance around, getting in their way.

'This way to the dining-room. I'm banning Amelia from going in there.'

'Thanks,' Sarah-Louise murmured. Pity she couldn't ban the child from her party.

The dining-room was rather posh with 15 chairs round a large table. Good job she'd brought two table-cloths. Olly was piling the boxes on the table and Sarah-Louise was beginning to get a bit flummoxed. She needed to lay the table only it was getting covered with things.

'That's lovely, thanks, Olly. If you could put the two boxes of clothes and party bags on the floor over there, that will be fine.'

'Do you want me to anything else?' he asked.

'Think I'll be fine now. Thanks so much. I'll give you a call later, if that's still OK?'

'Course. I'll be off now.' He leaned over and kissed her cheek. 'Bye then.'

'Bye. And thanks again.'

He left her to it, as she hoped he

would. Her plan was to set up everything here and then organise some party games. Get the little darlings weary enough to sit down and enjoy their tea. Then she'd do some magic tricks and entertain them with that and bring Molly in for petting.

Hopefully after that, the parents would come back to collect their children and take them home. She hadn't actually discussed the length of the party with Mrs Treswillian so hoped she wasn't too far out with the timing.

She moved the boxes on to one of the chairs and found the tablecloths. They only just covered the table. Then she put out the plates and napkins and in the centre, she put the birthday cake. Pity she didn't have a sort of stand for it so it would look more inspiring.

Soon, she had put out sandwiches, sausages and crisps and all the rest of the things. Jellies were set out and pizzas set to warm in the oven. It looked a good table, she was thinking.

Mrs Treswillian popped her head round the door to make sure she had everything she needed.

'Thanks, I think so.'

'Jolly good. Evidently one of the children is allergic to eggs so please make sure she doesn't eat anything with eggs in, will you?'

'Oh, dear. She won't be able to have any birthday cake or small buns. I think most of the rest is OK.'

'Sorry, I should have warned you before. I'll see if I can find some biscuits or something she can have.'

She disappeared again and Sarah-Louise wondered how her battle was going to get Amelia to change.

There was a ring at the doorbell. The afternoon was really beginning. She closed the door to the room and went through to the hall. Several small girls were standing around clutching parcels, looking very nonplussed.

'Come through to the lounge,' Sarah-Louise invited. 'I'm not sure where Amelia is but I'm sure she'll be down in a minute.' They were all completely tongue-tied and nobody spoke a word. 'My name is Sarah-Louise. Are you going to tell me your names?'

'Sacha,' one of them whispered.

'Jonquil,' another said. The rest said nothing. The doorbell rang again.

'Some more people are here,' Sarah-Louise said brightly. 'We'll soon have enough to play a game.'

'What game?' the one called Sacha asked.

'Musical bumps,' Sarah-Louise replied off the top of her head.

'That sounds good.'

The bell rang again so she went out to see if someone was letting them in. She opened the door and two more little girls came in.

'What time do you want us to pick them up?' the mother asked.

'About five-thirty to six o'clock, if that's OK.'

'Fine. We'll see you then. Enjoy yourselves, girls.'

Sarah-Louise shepherded them into the lounge.

'What are your names?' she asked.

'Mandy and Veronica,' one of them said.

'Hello, Mandy and Veronica. I'm sure you all know each other, don't you? I'm just going to look for Amelia and her mummy.' She went into the hall.

'Mrs Treswillian?' she called. 'Several of Amelia's guests are here, if she's ready to come down.' Five more are due, she was thinking. The doorbell rang again.

'Hope you don't mind. Jayne's little sister's come as well. She does know Amelia and I felt sure she'd be welcome.'

'Oh, yes, of course,' Sarah-Louise murmured. Just what she didn't want to happen. She did have extra plates but it was the party bag that would be a problem. Oh well, she'd solve that one later.

'Come on in, girls, and leave your coats in the hall.' She took them into the lounge to the rest of the group.

'Would you like to put the presents you've brought on this table here? Then we can begin to play some games.' This was not going to be the easiest party she had ever done.

It certainly was the first time the hostess had refused to come down. Usually the child was bouncing round like a maniac . . . just as Amelia had been when they were unpacking the car. Now it had gone strangely quiet.

The last little girls arrived and so she started to organise the party games, hoping Amelia would come down at some point soon.

Musical bumps went down very well. They all got giggly and tension eased.

Traditional Oranges and Lemons was next and Hunt the Thimble provided shrieks of joy when someone noticed it on top of a small felt creature Sarah-Louise had brought from home.

At last, the door opened and Amelia stood there, her face rather red and blotchy from the tearful exchange she'd had with her mother. She was dressed in jeans and a T-shirt rather than a party dress.

'Hello, Amelia,' one of the girls said.

'I've brought you a present,' one of the others said.

'Ooh, goody. Where is it?' The child's mood was rapidly passing and she became her usual self. She tore at the carefully wrapped parcels and tossed everything to one side as it was revealed.

'Aren't you going to thank everyone for bringing you such nice presents?' Sarah-Louise said. She couldn't bear to see the such bad manners.

'Yes. Thanks, everyone. Now what are we going to play next?'

'Pass the parcel,' the party planner said. She had wrapped it so that everyone would get the chance to peel off a layer of paper and find a balloon. 'OK, sit on the floor in a circle. When the music stops, you unwrap a layer till you get to the middle.'

The game went well until Amelia

pulled off two layers before the music could start again. That meant one child would miss out.

'I've got two balloons,' the birthday girl yelled.

A few more games followed until they were all panting and looking weary. Now was the time for tea. They were all instructed to wash their hands in the cloakroom and then to wait for everyone to be finished.

'OK, everyone. Tea is through here.' They all trooped through the double doors and sat down. Sarah-Louise whisked out another plate and napkin and asked for another chair to accommodate Jayne's little sister.

She had forgotten about the party bag problem and decided that Amelia didn't really need one. She could hand them out to her guests instead.

'It's fine,' Amelia's mother said when sarah-Louise mentioned it. 'I've got one more present I was saving for later. To help get her to go to bed, actually. I'll put it in the kitchen ready.'

'Thanks so much. I'm sorry it happened but when an extra child turned up, well, it did throw me a little.'

'Looks as though you've done a splendid job on the tea. Most of it seems to have gone. Are you ready for the birthday cake now?'

'I think so. I'll light the candle and then they can all sing.'

The traditional song sounded a bit off with everyone hitting different notes. Amelia sat staring at the candle and joining in with the singing, on and off. Then she blew out the candle and everyone clapped.

'There should have been six candles really,' she complained.

'One big one instead of lots of them. So you could all see the picture on the cake.'

Several of the children decided they didn't want anything else so their portions were wrapped in napkins to take home.

'I'll clear up later,' Sarah-Louise said to the mother. 'I think it will be best to get them in the other room and I'll do some magic tricks. OK, everyone into the lounge and find yourselves a seat.'

She put the cloak on and carried her box into the lounge.

She remembered Olly and went back to call him. He said he would come round right away. She went and performed her tricks, all fairly simple but the children loved it — that is, all except Amelia.

'I saw how you did that,' she announced. 'It isn't magic at all.'

'Perhaps you'd like to come and help me with my next trick,' Sarah-Louise suggested. 'I need someone to be sawn in half. Will you do it?'

'No!' the birthday girl shouted. 'I'm not going to be sawn in half.' She looked as if she might burst into tears.

'OK, well sit quietly and I'll forget it.' Sarah-Louise saw Olly park the car and decided it might be time to introduce the dog. She hoped Molly would co-operate and behave herself.

'Right, then. Amelia, I'd like you to hold up this sheet. Could some of you others help her? That's right. I'm now going to make a spell to invite a huge dog to appear behind this sheet.' She muttered a spell and the door opened and in came Molly.

'Drop the sheet.' There were immediately cries of delight. The dog wandered amongst them, wagging her plumy tail at getting so much fuss.

'Is it for me to keep?' Amelia asked. 'I want it. It can stay in my room.'

'No, I'm afraid not. She's just come for a party visit.'

'Can we stroke her?' one of the girls asked.

'Of course you can. But be gentle and don't shout at her or she'll think she's been naughty.'

There was a ring at the doorbell and much to Sarah-Louise's relief, it was the first parent come to collect her child.

Sarah-Louise grabbed the party bags and got Amelia to hand them out. They all had a piece of cake added to them by Mrs Treswillian.

In all the excitement, Molly lay down and seemed to have gone to sleep. Thank goodness, the anxious organiser thought.

When the final child had gone, Sarah-Louise sighed with relief. She went back into the dining-room and began to load the plates into a dustbin sack.

Olly helped her, munching the odd sausage and sandwich. There was still lots of bits left so she put them on to clean plates and left them on the table. Soon, everything was tidy and she was ready to leave.

'Thank you so much,' Mrs Treswillian said. 'I think it all went splendidly. I'll certainly tell my friends about your good work. I hope it will mean more parties for you to organise. Now, I think we said three hundred, didn't we?'

'Yes, thank you.'

'I'm going to give you more than you asked for, for all the extras you brought.

I'm sure it must have cost you lots to do such lovely party bags and the cake, and so on.'

'That's great. Thank you very much.'

'I'll write a cheque if that all right.'

'Of course. Thank you.'

As they drove away, she lay back in Olly's car and told him she wanted to sleep for a week.

'I'm not surprised. I can think of easier ways of earning a living.' He grinned.

Late-night Emergency

Once back at the flat, they unloaded everything from the car and dumped it in the kitchen. Sarah-Louise flopped down on the sofa.

'I'd better just go and get Molly, if you don't mind,' Olly said.

'Course not. She knows this place pretty well. Make sure she has a bit of a walk first. Jeannie must be out somewhere. Goodness me, I'm exhausted.'

'Won't be long,' he said as he went out.

Sarah-Louise lay back and closed her eyes. She dozed off and didn't even hear him come back. Molly went over to her and licked her hand and she sat up with a jump.

'I could put the kettle on if you'd like some tea,' Olly offered.

'That would be great.' She smiled.

He went into the kitchen and came

back with a piece of paper.

Gone out with friends. Don't wait up . . . probably back pretty late. Jeannie. X

'That explains her absence at least. Wonder who she's gone with? School colleagues, I should think.'

'I could go and find a takeaway, if you like.'

'Olly, why are you so good to me?'

'I like you,' was his simple reply. 'So what's it to be? Chinese? Indian? Or something else?'

'I could go for a nice fattening pizza. Dripping with cheese. But you choose.'

'Sounds good to me. Do you want some tea while you wait?'

'No, it's all right. I'll clear away the stuff in the kitchen while you're out.'

'OK if I leave Molls here?'

'Course. I'll give her something to eat. I think there's some of her food left.'

Sarah-Louise washed the boxes from the party and left them to drain. Various other things she packed away in the cupboard she kept for party things.

Satisfied with the look of the place, she made some instant coffee and went to sit down. Olly came back and soon they were eating their pizzas.

'Gosh, I was starving. Never got round to eating lunch so I was certainly ready for that. You must let me pay for it.'

'Nonsense. I'd have suggested going out for dinner but thought you looked too weary.'

'I must work out how much I owe you. What was the bill at the super-market?'

'You kept it. I can't remember.'

'Whatever did I do with it? You paid it, so you must know.'

'I just put my card into the machine. I have no idea what was on it.'

'Oh, why am I so inefficient,' Sarah-Louise said, grabbing her bag and rifling through it. 'It isn't here. Are you sure you didn't have it?'

'Quite sure.'

'I thought you were supposed to be

an accountant? Surely you never sign credit card bills without checking on them?'

'Actually, you took the bill and I didn't see it. Look in your coat pocket.'

'Oh. Right.' She felt in the pocket and gave a grin. 'You were right. It's here.'

She uncrumpled it and peered down at it.

'One hundred and seventy-six pounds, and twenty pence. OK if I write you a cheque?'

'Course. I owe you for two days' dog minding so knock that off the bill.'

'Oh, are you sure?'

'Quite sure. I shall charge my sister when she comes back so please don't worry about that!'

'I can't imagine what it feels like to have enough money to pay bills and never worry about buying supper ingredients.'

'If you got a proper job with a proper wage, you'd be in the same position.'

Sarah-Louise grimaced.

'Trouble is, I have no qualifications or talents. I always seem to bumble around doing odd jobs that crop up.'

'I thought you went to uni?'

'No. I went to drama school but left after the first year and a half.'

'Why did you leave?'

'It wasn't really for me. All that deep breathing and projection of the voice. 'Speak to the person in the very back row' was always being thrown at me. Struck me that if they were hard of hearing they should sit nearer the front.'

Olly laughed.

'You are incorrigible. Did you leave on your own or were you thrown out?'

'Let's say it was mutual. Since then, I've been doing various odd jobs, including cooking dinner parties for wealthy people who can't be bothered to cook for themselves. Mind you, that's dropped off since the pound became worthless. Well nearly.'

'I think you mean since the recession.'

'Yes. Whatever.'

'And are you a good cook?'

'Reasonably. Usually fairly plain food but I can step up when necessary. Lots of people like fairly plain food in their homes. You know, school dinner puddings, that sort of thing. Or something lighter, if they prefer.'

'I could see if there's anyone at work who'd like you to cook their dinners. There are several fairly upmarket folks who might.'

'Really? That would be great. Gosh, I'm so glad you took me on to walk your dog.'

'She's had a busy day, too. It's time I was on my way,' Olly said, stretching and getting ready to get to his feet.

'I've got to write you a cheque,' Sarah-Louise reminded him. 'Hang on a mo. I have to find my cheque book. Oh, you won't pay it in immediately, will you? It won't clear if you do.'

'Leave it for now. It's on my credit card anyway so won't have to be paid for a while.'

'Thanks, if you're sure.'

'Course. Besides, it seems to make sure you see me again.'

'I thought you wanted me to have Molly again next week?'

Olly nodded.

'Well, yes, if you're willing. I can drop her off in the morning and collect her at night if that's OK?'

'I'm sure it will be fine.' Sarah-Louise grinned. 'I'd miss her if I thought she was going to be left at home on her own all day.'

'I had been going home in my lunch hour to let her out but it made it a dreadful rush. By the time I'd driven home and then got back to the office again, it really didn't seem worth it.'

'I should think not. Bring her round here and I'll look after her. She isn't really any trouble and she doesn't seem to shed a lot of hairs.'

Olly got up to leave, hesitated for a moment and then kissed her cheek. She smiled back at him. Then they both stood looking slightly embarrassed.

'Come on, Molly. Time to go home.' The large dog lumbered to its feet and wagging her tail followed him outside. 'See you on Monday.'

'Night, then,' Sarah-Louise replied.

It was half past ten and she decided it was time for bed. She felt utterly exhausted after her busy day and flopped down in her bed. Her brain was still in overdrive as she thought about her day.

She knew she would have liked Olly to be a bit more friendly and to have kissed her properly.

He did seem so very nice and also caring. Ideal in a boyfriend. She checked herself. What was she thinking? Boyfriend? She was his dog minder and nothing more.

He had helped her out with the party and he'd bought them meals on two evenings but that didn't really mean anything, did it?

Sarah-Louise turned over for the umpteenth time and tried to go to sleep. She heard the telephone ringing and groped for it on the bedside table but it wasn't there. It must be in her handbag.

She leaped out of bed, fearing the worst. It must be Jeannie calling for help, she thought. Nobody else would call her at this time.

She found the phone and answered it.

'Hi. Did I wake you?'

It was Olly.

'Not really. I couldn't find my phone. What's wrong?'

'Nothing. I wanted to hear your voice again. Couldn't sleep.'

'Oh. Well, nor could I, despite feeling utterly exhausted.'

'What are you doing tomorrow?'

Her heart raced for a second.

'Nothing, really. I usually clean on Sunday mornings. Well, we do it together and then have a large breakfast and then slump for the rest of the day.'

'We wondered if you'd like to go for a long walk? Me and Molly wondered, that is. I thought we could go to the beach somewhere. Molly loves the water and she would really enjoy the experience.'

'I don't see why not. Yes, that would be good.'

'We could have lunch in a pub I know. Dog-friendly, of course.'

'You always seem to be feeding me.'

'My pleasure.'

'I'll cook you a meal soon. Just to make up for it.'

'That would be lovely. OK then, I'll see you tomorrow. About eleven?'

'That's fine. I can even do my cleaning by then. See you tomorrow.'

'Bye. Sleep well.'

'And you. Bye.'

Sarah-Louise put the phone down beside her bed and lay smiling. It was nearly midnight but sleep still deserted her. She heard a noise and sat up.

It was Jeannie coming into the flat. There was a sudden crash and the sound of a curse. She must have fallen over something.

Sarah-Louise grabbed her dressing-gown and went into the lounge. Jeannie was sitting on the floor rubbing her leg.

'What's happened?'

'I tripped over something and now I can't stand up. I should have put the light on. I was trying not to wake you. Can you help me get up?'

'I'll try. You'll have to help a bit.'

'Ouch!' Jeannie cried. 'Goodness, I must have done more damage than I realised.'

'Try rolling on to this cushion,' Sarah-Louise said pulling a seat off the sofa. With a series of grunts and moans, Jeannie heaved herself up a little.

'Ouch!' she cried again. 'Whatever have I done to my ankle?'

'Don't know. Maybe it's dislocated or something. Shall I call for help?'

'Don't know. What time is it?'

'Nearly midnight.'

'Perhaps I should sit here till later. It may ease if I wait.'

'I'll go and get you a duvet or something. You don't want to get cold.'

97

'Thanks, love. How did your afternoon go?'

'Fine, thanks. Olly was wonderful. I really like him. I'm supposed to be going out with him tomorrow. I suspect I might be sitting at the hospital instead.'

'Hope not — but it's really painful at the moment.' Sarah-Louise could see her friend was suffering and stood looking at her, frowning.

'I think I'd better phone for an ambulance. There's no way I could drive you to the hospital. I couldn't get you into the car for one thing.'

'I don't like to make a fuss. I think it will probably improve.'

'Well, I don't. I'm going to phone right now.'

Sarah-Louise called the ambulance and explained the situation. She was told they were very busy but would get to her as soon as possible.

She asked if it was all right for her friend to have coffee.

'Better not. If it's broken and she

needs an operation, they won't be able to do it till it's worked out of her system.'

'That's what I thought. Thanks. I'll look out for them coming.'

She put the phone down and spoke to her friend.

'They'll be a while coming and I'm sorry but they advise not to have anything to eat or drink. How's it feeling now?'

'Very painful.' Jeannie shook her head.

'Help me take my mind off it. Tell me about your day.'

'OK. Well, we arrived at the house. It's a gorgeous place . . . '

Sarah-Louise went on for quite some time, telling Jeannie about the wretched birthday girl and her behaviour. She made Jeannie laugh a couple of times until she ran out of things to say about the day.

'What did you do this evening?'

'Ate pizzas. Olly fetched them from the shop and we chatted for ages. Then he took Molly home.'

There was a knock at the door.

'That must be the ambulance,' Sarah-Louise said, going to open the door.

'Paramedics,' the first man said. 'Where's the patient?'

'In here.' She ushered him through to the lounge.

'Hello. I'm Gerry. What's your name?'

'Jeannie.'

'OK, Jeannie. Just keep still while I take a look. What happened to you?'

'I don't really know. I came in and tripped over something in the dark. Ouch.'

After a minute or two the paramedic spoke again.

'Sorry, Jeannie, but I think you've possibly broken something. We'll need an X-ray to be sure. It may just be a bad sprain. I'll put a support on it and we'll take you in.'

'I'm so sorry. You must be very busy.'

'The usual Saturday night. Too many people drinking too much alcohol. Let's get you on to the chair and then into the ambulance.'

'Shall I come with her?' Sarah-Louise asked.

'Have you got a car? Otherwise you'll be stranded and taxis at this time of night are not really available.'

'Can I take yours, Jeannie?'

'Course. Keys are in my bag. It's on the table.'

For the next few minutes, the two paramedics were busy putting a support on her ankle and then fetching a sort of chair.

They explained what they wanted her to do and then set off towards the ambulance.

Sarah-Louise picked up the keys and having locked the door, followed the ambulance towards the main hospital.

She thought longingly of Olly lying in his bed fast asleep and wished she could do the same.

She would have to call him in the

morning to put him off for their outing.

The hospital was rather busy for the time of night.

'Look, I'm sorry to keep you up so late,' Jeannie said as Sarah-Louise sat down to wait with her. 'Do you want to go home? I can probably get a taxi back in the morning.'

'I'll wait till you've been seen. It might not have been broken and you'll want to get home quickly.

'Oh, here comes a doctor now.'

'Miss Clarkson? Can you tell me what happened?' He busied himself looking at her ankle, taking off the support plastic thing the paramedic had put on.

'I tripped over something and fell.'

'OK. I don't think it's actually broken but We'll get an X-ray to make sure. You'll certainly have a massive bruise there. Right. I'll organise that and see you later.'

He moved away briskly, carrying his folder of notes.

'I feel about this high,' Jeannie

moaned, using her thumb and fore-finger to show her what she meant.

'You were unlucky, love. Don't worry about it.' Sarah-Louise reassured her.

An hour later, Jeannie had had her X-ray and been cleared by the doctor. There was nothing broken but it was a bad sprain.

She had been given a long elastic sock and a pair of crutches and was told she could go home.

It was nearly six o'clock and both girls were feeling exhausted.

'Shall I get us a bacon roll from the hospital café and we can pretend it's breakfast?' Sarah-Louise offered.

'Sounds a brilliant idea. Oh, I haven't got any money. I left my bag at home.'

'It's OK. I'll pay for them. I've still got a bit of my dog money left.'

'Thanks. I'll pay you back. The least I can do.'

'Sit there then and I'll go and order something.' She went to the counter in the café but there was nobody there. It was machine coffee and sandwiches from another machine.

'Sorry, nobody's on duty. Shall we go home and I'll make us something?'

'Oh, dear. I suppose so. I did buy some bacon yesterday. I'll heave myself up again and make my way to the door. Can you fetch the car round? Can't face walking far.'

Sarah-Louise drove the car to near the door. More staff were coming in so it had to be a quick stop to pick up her friend. She mustn't forget to phone Olly and tell him what had happened.

She couldn't really see any way she could go out with him, sadly.

She stopped outside the flat to let Jeannie out and helped her to get inside and then went to park the car.

It was now seven-thirty and just about time to get up, she thought ironically. She gave a yawn and went inside to find Jeannie fast asleep on the sofa. All right for some.

She went into the kitchen to make some coffee and sat beside the bench to drink it. Perhaps if she went to bed now, she could be awake for when Olly planned to come. Decision made, she went to bed. She fell asleep as soon as she hit the pillow.

A Touch of Jealousy

At half-past eleven Sarah-Louise was still fast asleep and Olly was banging at the door. Jeannie hauled herself up and managing the crutches rather awkwardly, opened the door.

'Olly. How nice to see you.'

'Oh dear, what on earth have you been doing?'

'Only a bad sprain. Come in.'

'Do you mind if I get Molly? I'm assuming Sarah-Louise is getting ready?'

'For what?'

'We're supposed to be going out for the day.'

'Oh. I don't know where she is. We were at the hospital most of the night. I suppose she's gone to sleep.

'I fell asleep on the sofa so maybe she's in bed. Shall I go and see?'

'I don't like to put you to the trouble.

You're obviously having difficulty walking anywhere. Why don't you sit down and I'll make us a cup of coffee?'

'Do you mind?'

'Course not. I'll put the kettle on and go and get Molly. Tell you what, I could send Molly in to wake her up.'

'Good idea,' Jeannie said with a laugh. 'I must sit down again. I could do with a coffee.'

'Then I'll make it right away.' He gave her a polite a bow and went out to fetch his dog.

By the time Sarah-Louise awoke, it was almost noon. She came through from the bedroom clad in her shortie nightie and found Jeannie and Olly laughing hilariously at some joke.

Molly lifted her head and wagged her tail at the sight of her.

'Oh, you're awake at last,' Jeannie said.

'Don't let me interrupt you,' Sarah-Louise said with a hint of sarcasm.

'Hi there, you. How are you today?' Olly asked.

'Apart from very little sleep, I guess I'm all right. My friend here kept me up all night but I expect she's told you all about that.'

'Perhaps you should get dressed,' Jeannie suggested.

'Oh. Yes, I suppose I should.' She turned to Olly. 'Sorry I didn't ring you but I didn't think you'd be up at that time.'

'I'm usually up by six-thirty. I take Molly for a walk and then come back and make breakfast.'

'Goodness, that sounds incredibly healthy,' Jeannie said. 'I bet you always eat very healthily, too.'

'Not really. I enjoy food and don't seem to put on weight.'

'OK, well I'll leave you two to discuss diets and go and dress.' Sarah-Louise felt annoyed that nobody was interested in her and stomped off to her room.

Heavens, Olly was her friend after all and the two of them seemed to be getting on famously. She hated feeling jealous but she knew she did.

The two of them both had jobs and she was the odd one out. Stupid thoughts raged round her head.

Anyway, she could hardly go out with Olly and leave Jeannie on her own. She dressed in some elderly jeans and pulled on a T-shirt.

No point dressing too smartly if she was only staying at home.

'Do you want some coffee?' Olly asked. 'I seem to be coffee maker in chief.'

'Oh, well, yes, thanks.'

'I won't have any more,' Jeannie said. 'I need to go to the bathroom. If you could hang on to the crutches while I pull myself up . . . ' she said to Sarah-Louise. 'I will get used to it, I'm sure.'

She made what seemed a huge effort to stand up and clutched her friend as if she was going to fall.

'It's OK, love. Here you are.' Sarah-Louise handed her the crutches and watched as Jeannie tottered from the room. It seemed as if it was going to be a difficult time for her.

At least today was the first day and it must get better after that. Sarah-Louise couldn't help feeling sorry for her friend despite the odd pangs of jealousy.

'There you go,' Olly said as he came out of the kitchen. One steaming mug of coffee just how you like it.'

'Thanks. You seem quite at home here.'

'Thank you. It's your lovely homey sort of atmosphere. Very relaxing. My place seems sort of sterile and well, boring. Don't know why that is.'

'Obviously lacks the feminine touch.'

'But this place you said was rented? Was it furnished?'

'No. It's all our stuff in here. Oddments we picked up at different times. I already had lots of catering sort of stuff. Baking tins and so on.'

'Well, whatever, it does work pretty well. Perhaps I should follow your example and pick up a few oddments.

'Look, I'm assuming our trip out is

off? You can't really leave Jeannie on her own, can you?'

'I'm really disappointed but no, not really. We could take Molls for a walk but I'll have to come back and do something to eat.

'You're welcome to stay if you want to. It's a bit boring for you after planning a nice outing.'

'Outing? Who was having an outing?' Jeannie said coming back into the room.

'Well, we were. Me and Olly and Molly.'

'Go on, then. Off you go.'

'We can't leave you on your own. You can't even get a cup of coffee or anything.'

'Make me a flask. And a sandwich. I'll probably go to bed. I do feel very tired.'

'I don't know,' Sarah-Louise muttered. 'I'm not sure I'd be happy to leave you alone.'

'Oh, for goodness' sake. I'm not a child. You go out and enjoy yourselves and leave me in peace. I'll be fine.'

'Are you sure?' Olly added.

'Quite sure. Go on, the pair of you.'

'Three of us, actually. I need to change. I'm dressed for staying at home.'

'I'll make Jeannie's supplies while you change,' Olly offered. 'Go on. Get glammed up. Or at least change out of those scruffy jeans.'

'Yes, sir,' Sarah-Louise said with a laugh as she went into her bedroom.

She selected a newer pair of jeans and pulled on a smart top. A quick touch of make-up and she was ready.

'There are some sandwiches and I've put coffee in the flask,' Olly said to Jeannie.

'Thank you — now go on, get out of here.' Jeannie grinned and waved them away.

It was rather breezy outside so they both pulled on anoraks and went out to Olly's car. Molly was heaved into the back and they set off.

'I thought we'd go along the south

coast and down to the Lizard, if that's all right.'

'Great. Haven't been down there for ages. There's lots of places for Molly to run around, too.'

'I thought we'd go to Church Cove for a while and then stop at the pub on the way back. They let dogs in so she won't have to stay in the car.'

'Sounds wonderful. This is such a treat, especially after yesterday.' She gave a slight shudder at the memory of the spoilt child whose party it was.

'I quite enjoyed myself, actually.'

'You weren't there for the start of everything. But let's forget about it all and enjoy today.'

They drove the few miles along the road towards the Lizard Peninsula and down past Culdrose airbase. He turned off and went down a twisting road towards the sea.

'Don't think I've been down here before.'

'It ends near a beautiful beach where dogs are allowed to run. There aren't all that many dog-friendly beaches left in Cornwall.

'You need to know where they are. That's the pub I was thinking of for lunch,' he commented as they drove past.

'Nice. It looks quite old.'

'Oh, it is. The food is good there. I fancy a nice steak pie and chips. Or maybe some fish. I'll see after we've walked.'

They parked next to a farm and walked along a somewhat smelly road. Molly was in heaven, pulling on her lead and sniffing where the cows had been.

'Goodness, I haven't seen her this lively before. It's usually a case of me leading and her vaguely following.' Sarah-Louise was smiling and feeling very happy.

She felt slightly ashamed of her feelings of jealousy with Olly and Jeannie. They obviously got on well and he was such a lovely guy, he seemed at ease with everyone.

'Slow down, girl,' Olly called out to his dog. 'I can't walk that fast. You'll pull me over. She recognises where she is and she's excited to see the beach.'

'Gosh . . . I'm amazed to see such enthusiasm. I always thought she was such a quiet dog.'

'You just wait till she's near water. She goes mad. Hope there aren't too many small people on this beach as she is rather big and possibly scary.'

They came to the ramp that led down to the beach and Molly was completely over the top with excitement.

Olly let her off the lead and she bounded away, barking madly.

Molly ran straight into the sea, jumping over the waves and swimming back out again. She gave a massive shake and water droplets flew into the air. Then she bounded back to the pair and miraculously, she was almost completely dry.

'She's amazing. How can she feel so dry after bounding through so much sea water?'

'It's the breed. They're used as rescue dogs in some places. You know, surfer dogs sent out to help surfers in difficulties.

'Their coats are quite oily and so don't absorb water. Amazing swimmers, too. They have sort of webbed paws that help them swim really well.'

'Wow. OK, you've sold her to me. Where did you find out all that?'

'Looked it up when my sister bought her. She is such a lovely dog and so loyal, too. Good job I knew her well before I got myself lumbered.'

Molly ran into the sea again and obviously loved it. She ran along the edge and almost dived into the waves. They both stood there watching her and laughing at her pleasure. She came out again and ran up to them, shaking like crazy.

'Get away, you horrible wet thing,' Olly complained.

The dog ran towards Sarah-Louise who ran round and sheltered herself behind Olly.

'Come on, you,' Olly said. 'Run around a bit to dry off the surface and then we'll go and eat.' He produced a ball from his pocket and threw it for the dog to chase. She ran after it and left it on the sand where it had landed.

'Typical. I'll go and fetch it myself.' The dog bounded after him, barking in excitement.

He threw the ball back to where Sarah-Louise was standing and she managed to catch it.

Olly and the dog came back to her and soon they were both laughing. He took her hand and suggested they abandon the beach and go back to the car.

'What's the little church?' she asked, noticing it tucked in a corner near the cliff.

'We can go and look at it if you want to. Molly can't go in, of course, but I can tie her up to something.'

The two of them went inside. It was a small place, obviously used regularly and had a wonderful old ceiling on one side.

It was carved with pale wood and looked as if it had been there for many centuries.

'Wow, just look at that,' she murmured, gazing up at it. 'Amazing.'

They went outside and were greeted by an ecstatic Molly who had not liked being tied up one little bit.

'The tower with the bells is over there,' Olly said, indicating the separate building.

'I wonder why I've never been here before?' Sarah-Louise said. 'It's so lovely. And the beach over there. It's a different world. What's the building on the top over there?'

'An old people's home.'

'Wow, what a place to be. I wouldn't mind being old if I could live somewhere like that.'

They wandered back along the road to where they had parked, chatting all the way.

Olly was so easy to talk to, she was

thinking. It made such a change from most of the people she usually met at kids' parties.

Mind you, they were usually fathers who had little time to spend with their children and large enough incomes to afford her services.

'So, what do you think?'

'Sorry?

'Do you think we should take something back for Jeannie?'

'What sort of something?'

'Food, of course. She won't be able to cook anything and she'll need a proper meal won't she?'

'I'll knock up something later.'

'But they do proper meals to take away at the pub. We could take a pie ready to cook in the oven and a plate of vegetables to warm through.'

'I suppose so. Hadn't really given it much thought. I was thinking of something like an omelette. She probably won't want a lot.' Sarah-Louise felt that twinge of jealousy again.

Olly was obviously thinking about

her flatmate and seemed concerned about her welfare.

'I just felt concerned about her, that's all,' he said.

He had confirmed her very thoughts. She gave a shrug.

'Please yourself,' she muttered. He gave her a sharp look but said nothing.

'Come on then, Molly dog. Get into the back.' The large dog lumbered into the car and settled down with a deep sigh. She was weary after her exciting time on the beach.

They drove the short distance to the pub and went inside. They left Molly in the car as she showed no sign of wanting to go inside with them.

'Wow, what a lovely place. Really cosy, isn't it?'

'Thought you'd like it. Hi, there,' he spoke to the lady behind the bar then turned to Sarah-Louise. 'What do you want to drink?'

'I'd like a shandy, please. I feel really thirsty.'

'OK and I'll have a beer and the

lunch menu, please.' They went to sit on the comfy side benches and peered at the menu.

'There's a specials board over there. I might go for one of those — although their steak pies are wonderful too. Decisions, decisions.'

She laughed.

'My problem, too. Think I'll go for one of the fish dishes. They sound wonderful.'

'Their fish and chips is amazing, too.'

'Sounds as if you've been here quite a lot.'

'I suppose I have. We come here with the office crowd whenever anyone is leaving or other special occasions. It's all good, really. Right. Steak pie wins. What about you?'

'I'm going to stick with the second fish special, please. Can I share the bill with you?'

'I invited you out so no, thank you. Nice to have a woman who doesn't take everything for granted, however. I'll go and order.'

She smiled, slightly relieved that she wasn't going to pay. She hadn't yet put the money from the party in the bank so was short of ready cash.

She also needed to pay Olly for his share of the bill for food and party bags.

The rest of the money would have to go towards the rent. Why was life so difficult?

He came back to sit beside her. She smiled at him and he took her hand and gave it a squeeze.

She began to feel guilty again for suspecting him of fancying Jeannie. She was being so stupid, and she needed to snap out of it right away.

'I've ordered a pie to take home for Jeannie.'

'That's very kind of you. I'm sure she'll love it.'

The food was delicious and they both ate hungrily. They even had puddings and Sarah-Louise felt quite guilty at feeling so full.

'Think I need a long run now but that might give me indigestion so maybe I'll just sit.'

'Do you want another drink?' Olly asked.

'No, thanks. Nothing else. I feel very content now.'

'I'll go and pay and then we'll get on our way again. Need to let Molly out before we leave.'

She smiled and nodded. Olly paid for their meals and was given a carrier bag to take home.

He peered inside and gave a nod. It was beautifully wrapped for carrying home with no chance of spillage.

'This is really well done,' he said to Sarah-Louise.

'Excellent. It's a good service, isn't it?'

'I haven't used it before but saw it on the poster. I know various pubs do it for elderly folk who live nearby, but this is a bit different.'

An excited Molly bounded out when they got back to the car. She looked around for the beach again, ready to go and play in the waves.

'Sorry, girl. You've had your beach time for today. Go on, do what good dogs should do and we'll get on our way.'

They didn't hurry too much, driving across the Lizard Peninsula and looking at the huge satellite dishes that communicated with the rest of the world. Then they went back towards Truro and eventually arrived back at the flat.

'Hello,' Sarah-Louise called softly, 'are you awake?'

'Thank goodness you're back,' Jeannie's voice came from her bedroom. 'Come in. I've fallen again and can't get up.'

'Oh, Jeannie, what on earth were you doing?'

'I wanted to lie down and when I got in here, I fell again.'

'But how long have you been lying there?'

'Dunno. Lost all track of time. Not long after you left. I'm so stiff. I've tried to get up but I'm stuck here and my crutches are over there.'

Jeannie was lying on the floor between a chest of drawers, her wardrobe and the end of the bed.

'I'd never believe it would be so impossible to move.'

'Oh, you poor thing. I'll get Olly to come and help. I can't lift you by myself. Olly?' she called. 'Can you come in here, please?'

'Oh, goodness. What's happened?'

The two girls explained.

'OK, so you need help in getting up. Sarah-Louise, you go the one side and I'll get the other. Not much room to move but if we both haul at the same time and Jeannie pushes with her good leg, I think we should manage it.'

They both heaved at the same time and the patient rose up.

'OK. I'll pass you the crutches and you can get back into the other room,' Olly said.

'Thanks, both of you. I felt so stupid, getting stuck like that. I could do with one of my sandwiches now. And I'm gasping for a drink.'

'We can do better than sandwiches. We've brought you a proper dinner. Just needs heating up.'

'Oh wow, that's terrific. Thank you so much.'

'I'll go and put the oven on. It'll take about twenty minutes.'

Sarah-Louise left them in the lounge and went into the kitchen. She unpacked the meal and saw it was all in containers that could go straight into the oven. She made three mugs of coffee and took them through.

Olly was sitting on the arm of the sofa, where Jeannie lay spread out. They looked very comfortable and seemed to be getting on very well indeed.

'Just telling Jeannie about Molly's escapades in the sea.'

'She sounds like quite a character. Where is she by the way?'

'Still in the car. Thought I'd better leave her there. Don't want you tripping over her.'

'Why not bring her in? She'll

probably just, lie down anyway. It's a shame to leave her on her own.' Jeannie smiled up at him.

'OK. Thanks. Maybe I should get back home before too long.'

'Oh, please stay on. You'll cheer me up.' Jeannie was adamant.

'Well, if you're sure I'm not a nuisance. Thanks. I'll go and get Molly.'

Sarah-Louise smiled and raised her eyebrows slightly. It seemed her friend was almost trying to flirt with Olly.

Happy Ending?

It was a pleasant evening but Sarah-Louise was still feeling unreasonably jealous of her flatmate. She tried to stamp it out of herself but then Jeannie would say something outrageous and made Olly laugh. She'd heard most of Jeannie's jokes and stories before — usually when her friend was really flirting with someone.

'We should go out together one night. Haven't you got a friend you could bring with you so there'd be a foursome?'

'Several people in the office would be pleased to come with us. I'll fix it and let you know. But you'll have to get better first. Can't have you limping around and falling over.'

'I'm sure with a bit strong arm to support me, I'd be fine. I'll have to take some time off school so I shall definitely need cheering up by the evening.

'Do say you'll come round tomorrow.' Jeannie was beginning to enjoy her sprained ankle now she was comfortably sitting and the painkillers had kicked in.

'I won't promise to take you out tomorrow but I'll certainly come round to see you both.

'In fact, if I bring Molly round tomorrow, I could stay on after I come to collect her. How about that?'

'I'll cook us something,' Sarah-Louise said. 'I can pick something up when I walk Molls.'

'Excellent. All arranged nicely. Now, I think it's time I went to bed. Can you help me?' Jeannie asked.

'What me?' Olly said, in surprise.

'No, of course not. Go home, young man. None of that sort of thing here, thank you very much,' Sarah-Louise said.

'Shame. I'll see you in the morning, assuming you're still willing to Molly-sit.'

'Course. I'll look forward to it.'

'Come on, then, girl. Let's go home again. It's becoming a bit of a habit being here, isn't it?'

'Thank you again for today. It was lovely,' Sarah-Louise told him.

'My pleasure. We must do it again, perhaps the three of us.'

She let him out and locked the door behind him. She leaned against it and wished she didn't feel so deeply for him. She had quite thought he was going to be the One.

He was kind and thoughtful and always seemed willing to help. Perhaps she was simply feeling jealous because of that.

Perhaps he wasn't her knight in shining armour after all.

But she did like him such a lot, and hadn't he held her hand? Or at least given it a very friendly squeeze.

'Right, madam. Let's get you off to bed. If you sit down on the bed, I'll help you undress.'

Jeannie hobbled through to her

bedroom and flopped down on the bed.

'Think I'm getting the hang of these crutches now,' she muttered. 'Blooming things. He's really nice, isn't he? Your Olly?'

'My Olly? He's very helpful and seems to be caring.'

'Oh, yes. Bringing me that meal was so kind. It was delicious, too. Didn't know pubs would do that sort of thing.'

Sarah-Louise got Jeannie a glass of water and left it beside her bed, along with the packet of pills she had been given at the hospital.

Apart from feeling slightly annoyed with her flatmate, she really was fond of her and felt very sorry for her — just as long as she kept away from Olly.

She realised she felt absolutely shattered and went to bed herself. She fell into a dreamless sleep and slept solidly till almost eight o'clock the next morning.

Once she realised the time, she shot out of bed and went through to see how Jeannie was.

'I've got to phone school and tell them I'm not going in,' was the first thing she said. 'I suppose you couldn't call them for me? Might sound better coming from someone else.'

'I'd better get dressed first.'

'Why? It's not a video phone. Nobody can see you.'

'I know that but Olly will be here soon with Molly. I don't want to scare the poor bloke off with me in my nightie.'

'Just go and phone for me first. Please, one of the secretaries will be there. She always goes in at eight to take any calls.'

'Oh, all right, then.' Sarah-Louise went and called Jeannie's school. It was engaged. She tried again, seconds later.

She glanced at her watch. It was getting closer to Olly's arrival. She tried once more and was about to give up when someone answered.

'Hello,' Sarah-Louise said. 'I'm calling on behalf of Jeannie Clarkson. I'm afraid she's sprained her ankle and so won't be in for a few days.'

'Oh, my gosh. We've got so many staff off at the moment. Some bug that's going round. Are you sure she can't get in? Maybe she could just sit in front of her class?'

'I'm sorry, but I really don't think she's up to it at the moment. I'll pass on your concerns and see how she is later in the week. She says she's very sorry.'

'Oh, all right. Hope she feels better sooner rather than later. Thanks for your call.'

Sarah-Louise put the phone down and went to tell Jeannie the latest.

'She is a bit of a fuddy-duddy, that one. Hates it when her little routine is upset. I couldn't possibly go in and manage a class like mine.

'You really need to be on top of everything with that lot. There are at least four troublemakers amongst them.'

'OK, well, I'm going to dress now. I'll sort breakfast after Olly's been.'

Sarah-Louise rushed into her bedroom and found some slightly grubby jeans and a top that normally should have been in the wash a week ago.

She brushed her hair quickly and went through to the kitchen to put the kettle on. If she didn't have some coffee fairly soon, she'd never even begin to feel human. There was a knock at the door.

'Morning. How's the invalid?' Olly said with a smile.

Molly pushed past him and settled down on the carpet with a deep sigh.

'I think she's OK. I haven't really had time to ask her. She was too busy making me phone her school to tell them she couldn't go in.'

Sarah-Louise suddenly noticed there was something different about him. 'You're not wearing glasses today.'

'Contact lenses for a change.' Olly smiled and Sarah-Louise decided he looked equally attractive with or without this glasses.

'Looks like Molly is happily settling

down already,' he added.

'Course she is. This is her second home for now.'

'Sorry, I must get off or I'll be unforgivably late. Still OK for tonight?'

'Yes, of course. Look forward to seeing you later.'

'Love to Jeannie,' he called back as he dashed down to his car.

She went back into the kitchen, made two mugs of coffee then took them into Jeannie's bedroom and sat down on the side of the bed.

'Molly's here,' she said unnecessarily.

'I gathered that. How was the lovely Olly?'

'OK, I suppose. Didn't say much but he sent his love to you.'

'That was nice of him.'

'He asked how you are but I was so involved with phoning your school I forgot to ask. How did you sleep?'

'Sort of OK. I kept waking up and then couldn't get comfortable.'

'What can I do to help?' Sarah-Louise asked.

'Pass me the crutches once I've got my feet on the floor.'

She watched as Jeannie manoeuvred herself round to work her way to the edge of the bed. Sarah-Louise held her crutches and the girl took them and heaved herself up.

'What are you going to wear? I'll get it out for you.'

'I was going back to bed, actually.'

'Oh. I assumed you'd stay up now you're on the move. You can put your leg up on the sofa.

'I've got to take Molly for a walk fairly soon so make your mind up.'

'I'll get up if it's easier for you.'

'Well, it probably would be.'

Why should she stay in bed all morning while being waited on hand and foot?

Sarah-Louise realised she wasn't being rational and that it was Olly's fault for sending his love to her friend.

She grabbed the bread and dropped four slices into the toaster. That was it for bread so she needed to get some more.

She started a list. Fortunately, Jeannie had been shopping on Saturday so they had lots of basics.

She needed something to impress Olly that evening. The toast popped up so she called out.

'Toast's ready, Jeannie. Do you need any help?'

'Think I'll manage, thanks.' Jeannie came into the kitchen and more or less balanced using the crutches and leaning against the unit.

'I'll bring it through to the sitting-room for you. What do you want on it?'

'Marmite, please.'

'Ghastly stuff.'

'Love it or hate it.'

'I'll bring the jar in and you can spread it yourself. I never know how much to put on. Go and settle on the sofa.'

Molly stirred slightly and lifted her tail in a token wag.

Jeannie went into the sitting-room,

flopped down and sat with her eyes closed. Sarah-Louise arrived beside her and pulled the small table across for her to put the toast down.

'Thanks a lot. I know it's a bit of a strain for you to have to do so much for me and I want you to know I'm very grateful.'

Sarah-Louise immediately felt awful for her thoughts and knew she must respond positively.

'Who else would help out? We're on our own, love, and it's no trouble. Let's make the most of a day or two of you at home and only a two or three walks with Molly to interrupt us.

'In fact, speaking of which, I'd better take her out now. I've just about finished my toast, have you?'

'Not really, but you go. I'll be fine.'

Sarah-Louise set off towards the park. She confided in Molly as she went and told her how upset she was feeling.

'It's your owner, you see. I thought he was so nice and friendly. I know it's silly as I've only known him for about a week but I thought he was going to be my special one.'

Molly looked up at her and wagged her tail.

'But then he met Jeannie and seems so friendly towards her, I don't think he even thinks about me. What do you think Molly?'

The dog wagged her tail again, as if she sensed her walker was unhappy.

'I see. So that's what you think about it all is it?'

They walked along by the river, quite near to Olly's office. She could see his car parked outside and smiled, just in case he was looking her way. They turned and walked back towards the flat.

'Now then, Molly. Can you sit outside the butcher's long enough for me to go in?' She fastened her lead to a convenient hook in the wall and went inside.

'Could I have a pound and a half of mince, please?' She had decided to make a lasagne for supper. Besides, mince was just about the cheapest thing she could afford.

She still hadn't put her cheque in the bank and just had some dog-minding money left.

'Thanks,' she said and went outside to collect Molly.

But she had disappeared. Her lead was still attached to the hook along with her collar.

'Oh heavens,' Sarah-Louise muttered. 'She can't have gone far but which direction?' She glanced up and down the road and went in one direction but there was no sign of her.

How on earth had she slipped her collar? Surely nobody would take her, not a dog of that sort of size.

Thoughts of dognappers raced through her mind. They were often giving out warnings. She felt a state of panic.

Whoever had taken her must have a large car or van and she had certainly not seen anything like that while she was in the butcher's.

'Excuse me,' she said to a passer-by,

'have you seen a large dog, a New-foundland. She's slipped her collar and got herself lost.'

'Sorry, not seen her, love.'

She asked several people going the other way but it seemed Molly had completely disappeared.

Perhaps she'd gone back to the flat. She did know that way, after all.

Sarah-Louise almost ran back to the flat but there was no sign of Molly anywhere. She burst into the flat and poured out her worries to Jeannie.

'I only left her for a few minutes while I went into the butcher's. When I came out, there was her lead and collar hanging there and no sign of the dog.

'Oh Jeannie, what will Olly say? And his sister? I must find her. Nobody would approach a dog of that size, would they?'

'Calm down. She must be some-where.'

'Yes, but where? Suppose she runs into the road? You know what the traffic's like. I'd better go and hunt some more.'

'I'm sorry I can't help. Take my car and drive round. She'll easily fit into the back.'

'Oh, that would be a help. Thanks.'

Sarah-Louise grabbed the keys and set off following the route she had walked. She drove round to the park but there was no sign of Molly. She simply didn't know where else to look.

She drove round several estates and finally parked or rather abandoned the car and went along the riverside.

Then she saw Molly. She was standing near to a black poodle, and looking, she thought, as if she were flirting with it.

'Molly, you naughty girl. Come here. I'm sorry, she's an real softie but I hope you weren't scared.'

'It seems she's taken a fancy to my dog. I was walking by and he stopped to sniff. Seconds later, she was following us. I did go back to look for you but you'd disappeared. I think she's fallen in love with Monty.'

'Oh, my goodness. He is lovely but Molly's a naughty girl. Come on then, you.'

Sarah-Louise put the collar and lead back on the dog and gave her a slight tug. Molly lay down and looked at her with a 'make me' sort of look.

'I'll come with you for a short while. I need to get back pretty soon anyway. I'm just exercising Monty for a friend who has a broken leg. You came from that way?'

'I'm afraid I sort of abandoned my car.'

Molly decided she would move if Monty was going and heaved herself up on her feet.

They came to the end of the river bank and there was her — or rather Jeannie's — car.

'I'd better move it quickly before a traffic warden turns up. Thanks for your help in making Molly move.'

'Think it was Monty who did it.

Perhaps we'll see you again sometime. Bye.'

'Bye. Hope to see you again.'

Sarah-Louise hoisted Molly into the car and climbed in herself. She spotted a traffic warden coming along the road and started it quickly and drove off.

'Phew. You wicked dog. Nearly caused me a nervous breakdown.'

Five minutes later they arrived back at the flat and parked the car in its usual place.

'Come on then, you,' she said to Molly. 'Let's go and see how Jeannie is getting on.'

'Hi. Did you find her?' Jeannie called.

'Eventually. She found a fella and went off with him.

'The owner of the other dog didn't realise she was following until it was too late. By the time she got back to the butcher's, I'd disappeared. I found them eventually anyway.'

'There was a call for you. I left the answering machine to take it. Another job by the sound of it.'

'Oh, good. I could do with a few more pounds in my coffers. Oh heck, I forgot to pay my cheque in. I'll see what the message says.'

'Hello. Can you do a party for my daughter a week on Saturday? What are your terms? She went to Amelia's party and has gone on and on about it. She adored the dog so can you bring it again?'

Sarah Louise established exactly what this mother wanted when she called her back. She wanted a full service like Amelia's party so she quoted the price she'd been given for previous party.

'That's fine. Thank you. Oh and the party bags . . . they were lovely. We'd like something similar, please.'

'And what sort of a theme would you like? I did a sort of magic presentation for Amelia but there are other things I can do.' She quoted circus, princess and a sort of interactive game show.

'I think possibly a princess sort of theme. My little Trudy is a very girlie sort of child. She'd like that.'

'Fine. And how many children are coming?'

'Ten at the moment but we haven't heard back from everyone yet. Is that a problem?'

'As long as I know a couple of days before, that will be fine.' After Sarah-Louise put the phone down, she did a punch into the air. 'Yes!' she called out.

'A good one, I assume?'

'Brilliant. Her little girl was at Amelia's party and insisted on having me there. Oh and she wants Molly, too. Hope Olly's willing to join me.

'Right, list time. At least I've got time to organise it all now. I do like parents who don't leave everything to the last minute.'

Sarah-Louise busied herself with a paper and pen and made a shopping list for the party bags.

'Perhaps I should buy a load of party bags ready for the future. I'll have to look into that.'

'Are we going to have something to

eat? It's nearly two o'clock and frankly, I'm starving. Do you want me to go into the kitchen and try to make a sandwich?'

'Don't be daft. No, I'll do it. What do you want?'

'I'd love some cheese on toast or is that too much to ask?'

'Course not. I'd better let Molly out first though or she'll burst. I've just realised I didn't let her go again after I put her in the car.'

Sarah-Louise felt she really must confess about Molly getting lost when Olly came round that evening.

She wondered whether she would lose her job if he was cross about it.

The lasagne was bubbling away in the oven, filling the whole flat with its savoury smell. Fingers crossed, that might help. He arrived at the door.

'Hello, ladies. Hi there, Molly. You been a good girl?' He petted the large dog and she rolled on to her back. 'You old softie. How are you feeling now, Jeannie?'

'A bit better, thanks. I can at least get up out of my chair and stagger along to the bathroom. If I can actually get there, I think I should be able to get back to school next week at the latest.'

'That's good news. And how are you, Sarah-Louise?'

'I'm OK, thanks. You?'

'Fine. What sort of a day have you had?'

'Molly ran off,' Jeannie burst out.

'Ran off? Never! For a start she never runs. Come on then. Tell me what happened.'

'I stopped at the butcher's and tied her securely to a sort of hook in the wall. It's specially designed for the purpose.

'A large poodle went past and Molly fell instantly in love. She pulled herself out of her collar . . . I know, how on earth . . . and walked after it.

'I panicked, thinking of all the roads she'd have to negotiate. I came back here to see if she'd miraculously found her way back and Jeannie lent me her car to drive around.

'Eventually I found her and the poodle sitting beside the river. Nice woman with the poodle.

'She'd been back to the butcher's but by then I'd left. So, I'm very sorry and I'll never even attempt to stop and shop when I'm with Molly.' She paused, waiting for him to say something.

'Sorry,' she added.

Change of Heart

'My goodness, you've certainly had an exciting day.'

'I'd hardly call it exciting. Worrying, more like.'

'Well, I'm glad you found her and I don't have to tell my sister the worst.'

'Do you want me to look after her tomorrow? Well, still look after her?'

'Course I do, you silly girl. I know it wasn't your fault. Now, what's this wonderful smell that's invading the flat?'

'Thank you so much. And I really am sorry. It won't happen again.' She flung her arms round him and kissed him on the cheek. He smiled.

'Can't get over her following a poodle, of all things.'

'It was a large one. A standard, I think they're called.'

'Bet she was still much larger. Oh

well, no harm done and Molly is in love. Now are we going to eat or are you going to drive me mad with the smell?'

It was a pleasant evening with all of them getting on very well. Sarah-Louise tried her best not to feel jealous and spoil anything but it was difficult.

She couldn't help noticing how much Jeannie laughed at things Olly said and how she seemed to hang on to his words.

Perhaps she should give up on him and leave him to Jeannie.

'I'll go and wash up,' she said, getting up and clearing the plates.

'Oh, by the way,' she asked Olly, 'are you busy next Saturday afternoon? I've got another party booking and they've requested a visit from Molly.'

'No, I don't think there's anything special happening. Molly enjoyed being petted at your last event.

'We'll be pleased to join you, won't we, girl?'

Molly wagged her tail but didn't

bother to get up.

'She definitely understands every word I say. Otherwise, would she wag her tail? I'll come and help with the washing up,' he offered.

'Don't worry, there really isn't much,' Jeannie said. 'Stay and talk to me. I've been so bored just sitting here on my own all day.'

'You fibber. You haven't been on your own. I've been here most of the day.'

'If I go and help, we'll both be back that much sooner. But I mustn't stay too long. I've hardly seen my place for the past few days. I need to do some washing as well.'

'You go if you want to. No need to help me. I can easily do the washing up.'

'Well, if you both don't mind, I really ought to go. I'll see you in the morning. Thanks again for dinner. It was lovely. Come on, Molly. Time to go. You must be starving.'

Sarah-Louise showed him out, rather hoping he might kiss her but not really expecting he would.

She closed the door and returned to the kitchen with a sigh. She had soon washed up and went into the living-room where Jeannie had put on the television.

'What are you watching?'

'Nothing really. Just put it on. Anything you want to see?'

'Wouldn't mind a look at that documentary that's on at nine. Other-wise, not really.'

'I might go to bed and read a bit.'

'As you like. Do you want some help?'

'I think I'll manage. I do feel much better. If you could drive me, I reckon I might manage at school in a couple of days.

'If I take a flask so I don't have to go down to the staff room for coffee and some sandwiches for lunch, I think I'll be OK.'

'Course I can drive you. It would have to be fairly early so I'm back for Molly but that's not a problem.'

Sarah-Louise felt cheerful for some reason at the thought of being alone during the day. She would plan what she was going to do for the party at the weekend in between looking after Molly and preparing the supper.

'So when do you want to go back?'

'Probably Wednesday but I'll see how I feel tomorrow.'

'OK. I'll tell Olly tomorrow. I'm sure I'll be back but I can warn him, just in case.'

'I do feel guilty about not being at school. It always means someone else has to look after my class.

'They can't always get supply teachers in. Maybe I will stay and watch the documentary with you. It does seem a bit early to go to bed.'

★   ★   ★

The days went by quickly. Jeannie decided to go back to school on Wednesday and left the car for Sarah-Louise.

She decided to go shopping and buy everything she needed for the party and also to do some shopping for the two of them.

Olly had his routine sorted and she was usually back from taking her flatmate to school when he arrived.

Sarah-Louise spent Thursday baking and preparing things for her party and the party bags were all packed and ready. She spent a little less on them for this occasion, as instructed. She was never usually this organised.

It made all the difference having the use of a car and she began to think about licensing her own car again, now she had a bit of cash.

'OK, Molly, time for you to go out,' she said to the dog on Thursday afternoon. Molly's tail lifted slightly as she tried to wag it. 'Come on, girl. You're getting rather lazy you know.' She put her lead on and tried to get her interested.

Molly just lay there, unwilling to move. Sarah-Louise tried to lift her body but couldn't do it at all.

'Come on, girl. Walkies,' she called excitedly. No response. 'Oh, come on, Molly. You must make a bit of effort.'

Nothing she could do would make the dog raise to her feet. Sarah-Louise knelt down and spoke to the dog quietly.

'Please come on, Molly. I've got to fetch Jeannie soon and if I haven't walked you first, you'll be most uncomfortable.'

Molly sighed and showed no sign of moving. Sarah-Louise had to accept the fact that Molly wasn't about to shift and hoped she would be all right when left alone.

Sarah-Louise sat outside Jeannie's school waiting for her friend. The children had all left and it was just the staff who were coming out.

She saw her flatmate at the door and started the car and drove as close to the door as possible.

'Thanks so much,' Jeannie said as she

panted her way into the car. 'Phew, I'm glad today's over.'

'Not feeling so good?'

'No it's not that. Just been a bit demanding, that's all. Home, James, and let me get a nice cuppa. Oh, where's Molly? Thought she'd be with you.'

'There's something wrong with her. She wouldn't or couldn't get up. I had to leave her lying there and come for you. I'm a bit worried about her.'

'Poor old Molls. What can it be?'

'No idea. I'll ring Olly if I still can't move her when we get back. Or maybe I should call the vet?'

'Olly first. You don't know which vet he uses. Come to think of it, he possibly doesn't even have a vet as she's his sister's dog.'

They stopped close to the outside door of the flat and Jeannie hauled herself out of the car. She was still using crutches but was managing much better now.

She waved Sarah-Louise away to

park in the car park and let herself into the flat.

'Hello, Molly. How are you, old girl?' Jeannie asked. The dog feebly wagged her tail and still lay where she had been for most of the afternoon.

'Come on then. Try to get up. If I can do it, you should be able to.'

Sarah-Louise arrived back.

'No movement,' Jeannie said to her friend. 'Nothing. She just about managed to wag her tail but she's very feeble.'

'Oh, I can't bear it. I'm going to call Olly right away.'

'Not sure what he can do. He doesn't finish work for at least another hour or two.'

'He might tell me which vet I should call. I can't leave her here, just lying. I don't even know if she's in pain or not.'

'She doesn't look as if she's in pain.'

But Sarah-Louise was already on the phone, waiting for Olly to answer.

'Olly? Sorry to bother you. It's Molly.'

'She hasn't run off again, has she?'

'Nothing like that. She's lying on the floor and simply won't get up. I've tried everything I can think of but she's just lying there. Her tail sort of quivers rather than wagging properly. Should I call the vet?'

'Leave it for a while. I'll come and look at her as soon as I can. Won't be long.'

'He's coming home soon,' Sarah-Louise told Jeannie. 'Well, coming here. He says wait for a while before calling the vet. 'Sorry, you wanted a cuppa. I'll put the kettle on.'

'Don't worry. That was just me being selfish.'

'I might as well. Nothing else I can do. So how was your day, apart from stressful?'

'All right, I suppose. I just had a problem with my disruptive kid who wouldn't stay in his place. I usually stand over him but I'm not up to that at the moment.

'In desperation I sent him to stand

outside the door and the Head came along and virtually scolded me in front of the whole class.

''If you can't control your children perhaps you need to take more time off.' That's what she said. None of the 'Good of you to come in' sort of thing.'

'Doesn't exactly sound very professional.'

'Professional? She doesn't know the meaning of the word. She is so awful as a Head. Don't know how she got the job in the first place. Probably knew all the right jargon to spout at the Governors.

'Sorry. Rant over. Do go and put the kettle on. You're right, I'm gasping.'

'Come on, Molly,' Sarah-Louise said again. She got down on her hands and knees and whispered in the dog's ear.

'What's wrong, girl? Why don't you get up?'

The dog made a slight noise in her throat. Sarah-Louise rose, shaking her head and went to make some tea. Jeannie looked at the dog and told her

160

to hurry up and get up.

'You're causing too much trouble you know. We could well do without it.'

'Sorry? I could hear your voice but not what you were saying,' Sarah-Louise shouted through from the kitchen.

'Just talking to the dog. Think Olly's here.'

'Oh, goodness. Right.' She went to open the door and Olly came in, looking worried.

'How is she?' were his first words.

'No change. She still won't move at all.'

'Hello, Molls. What's up with you?' At the sound of his voice, her tail wagged with a bit more energy than she had shown previously. 'Come on then, up you get.'

The dog made a huge effort and managed only to raise her head which then dropped dramatically with a thud. 'Heavens. Whatever's wrong with her?'

'I don't know. Shall we call the vet?'

'I think perhaps we should. I've never

seen anything like this. It's as if she's become incredibly heavy and can't even stand up. I don't have the vet's name with me.'

'I'll get the phone book.' He spent a few minutes looking through the list but no name came to him. 'Hang it, I'll call one of them and see who can come out. There's no way we can carry her out to the car. Has she eaten anything?'

'Not to my knowledge. I took her out this morning but haven't been able to get her to move since. She hasn't had anything to eat or drink since then.'

It took about half an hour for the vet to arrive. He asked all the same questions over again and still couldn't tell what was wrong with Molly.

'Seems very strange. Are you sure she hasn't eaten anything that could have disagreed with her?'

'Not since she's been in my care.'

'I'll have to take her into the surgery, somehow. Perhaps you can all help me to lift her? I'll go and get a sheet sort of thing to help and move the car closer to the door.' He left and the others stood there looking at the dog.

'Oh, dear. Poor Molly. What on earth can it be?' Sarah-Louise asked.

'Goodness knows. It must be something she's eaten.'

'Really, she hasn't eaten anything,' she protested, very close to tears by now.

The vet came back in with something that looked like a patient carrier.

'Right, if we can somehow slide this under her we shall then have something we can get hold of.'

He stood near her rear and pushed it under her, with Olly lifting as much as he could. It took a while but at last it was mostly underneath her.

'OK. If you can each grab a corner and we can all lift at the same time.'

'Sorry, I can't,' Jeannie wailed.

'Not to worry. Ready? One, two, three.' They all heaved together and somehow managed to lift her. They staggered towards the door and then outside towards his car or rather van.

Once they had managed to slide her inside, the vet closed the doors.

'Can you follow me to the surgery?'

'Of course,' Olly said. 'No need for you to come, Sarah-Louise.'

'Oh, but I'd like to. I'll just grab a coat and make sure Jeannie's all right.'

'Hurry up, then.'

She dashed inside and told Jeannie she was going to the vet's.

'I'm sure you'll be all right. I haven't done anything about supper yet. I'll get something on my way back.'

Olly was sitting in his car with the engine running ready to follow the vet and she climbed in quickly.

'Sorry. Don't think Jeannie was too pleased but I really am anxious.'

'Fortunately, my sister has insurance for Molly. Otherwise heaven knows how much the bill would be. I know insurance doesn't cover the whole cost but the important thing is to get her sorted. Hope you're ready for another big lift when we get there.'

They stopped outside the surgery

and the vet had already opened the back of the van.

'We'll go in this way. She hasn't moved at all so we can just put her on the table and I'll have a look at her.'

'Can we come in with you?'

'Well, you can certainly help get her inside but then you'll have to wait in the waiting room.'

They helped get her on to his table and then left the surgery to wait in the waiting room. Olly looked very worried. Sarah-Louise was almost crying but held it back.

Silently, the pair sat side by side, waiting and waiting. It seemed to take ages.

'This is driving me mad,' Olly snapped. 'He must have some idea of what's wrong with the dog.'

It must have taken almost an hour before anyone came out to speak to them. A nurse appeared at the door.

'I'm afraid we haven't been able to find anything wrong with her so far. We're going to do a CT scan, which means we shall have to shave off some of her fur. We've tried the hand-held scan but can't really see enough. She will have to be sedated, of course.'

'Please . . . do whatever you need to do for her. Goodness knows what she can have eaten. Obviously something that has disagreed with her.' He looked at Sarah-Louise and she stared down at her hands, which were clenched in her lap.

She felt his criticism of her looking after the dog and she felt it was unjust but said nothing.

'I'll bring you a form to sign to say you give your consent to any treatment. May I ask if you have pet insurance? Only this procedure is very expensive if you don't.'

'Yes, my sister bought it before she went away. I haven't got the forms with me.'

'No worries. Right. I'll go and get the consent form.'

'I'm so sorry,' Sarah-Louise muttered. 'I don't know what I could have done to make her so ill. She hasn't been left on her own at all today.'

'She's obviously picked up something and eaten it,' he said without a smile at all. Sarah-Louise felt dreadful and wondered if she really ought not to be there.

'She did run away from me yesterday but I don't think she ate anything then. I really am sorry,' she said again.

'Don't keep saying that. I know you didn't mean her to pick up something and eat it. But it looks as though she has.'

★　★　★

Olly had signed the consent form and was now pacing backwards and forwards. There were no other patients waiting at this time so the room was empty except for the worried pair.

'How long have we been waiting here?' he asked.

'About another hour, I suppose. Hope Jeannie's OK. I said I'd take fish and chips home for her . . . well, for our supper.'

'Go if you want to. No point in both of us staying here.'

'It's OK. I'll wait to know what's going on.'

'Suit yourself.' She cringed at his sharp tone. How could she have thought he was going to be her special man? OK, she knew he was worried but it could just have easily been something he had left out for Molly to eat or whatever. At last the vet came in.

'Sorry to keep you so long.' They both murmured something in response. 'We've done the scan and it looks as if there's a blockage partway before her stomach. It's something that looks pretty solid.

'I'm going to try to attack it from her throat but that may not work and I'll have to open her up. I'll go and get on with it right away.

'You don't need to wait. I suggest you go home and I'll phone when I've done the procedure. She'll need to stay here at least for the night. Hope that's OK for you both?'

'Thanks. Poor Molly. Hope you can do the simpler version.'

'So do I. Right. Make sure the nurse has your details.' He swept back into his surgery and they sat staring at each other.

'I'm so . . . '

' . . . sorry. I know. You've already told me that numerous times. Come on then. I'll drop you home and go and sit by my phone.'

'Won't you stay for some supper with us?'

'I think I'll go home, actually. I need to think how I'm going to explain this to my sister.'

'You should wait till you know Molly's going to be all right.'

'Maybe. Come on then.'

She didn't dare to ask him to stop to buy fish and chips and decided she'd go out again to fetch them.

It was now almost seven o'clock and she knew Jeannie would be worried. He stopped outside the flat and drove away again without saying a word. She went inside and found Jeannie in the kitchen.

'Hi. How is she?'

'I don't know. She having an operation at this very moment. She's eaten something that's blocked her . . . well just before her stomach, apparently.'

'Where's Olly?'

'He's gone home. I know he blames me and he could scarcely speak to me. I've said I'm sorry so many times. I really don't know what she can have picked up.

'I haven't got any fish and chips, either. I'll go and get some in a minute. I didn't dare to ask him to stop.'

'I was wondering whether to do omelettes? To save you going out again.'

'Could do. I feel hungry now. I don't mind going out.'

'OK. I must say I was looking forward to fish and chips. Won't take you too long, will it?'

Sarah-Louise drove out to the nearest

chip shop and bought their supper. She kept her mobile phone close by her so she could answer quickly. But it remained silent. They finished eating and still the phone didn't ring.

'Can't understand it. I really thought he'd have called by now. She can't still be in surgery, can she?'

'I've no idea. Perhaps you should call him?' Jeannie replied.

'Oh, I don't know. He was so angry with me.'

'How do you know it's your fault? She could have eaten something at his place.'

When it got to nine-thirty, Sarah-Louise could wait no longer. She dialled Olly's number and waited for him to answer. At last he did.

'Sarah-Louise? Thought it would be you.'

'What's the news?'

'Not good, I'm afraid. He's had to do a full-scale operation. He has managed to get it out but it's obviously been there for a while. It has begun to infect the surrounding area.'

'What was it? What on earth had she swallowed?'

'It was a sock. A smallish sock. I think it may have belonged to my sister's child.'

'But how on earth has she been eating and drinking?'

'It lodged to one side of her gullet and now the infection has destroyed part of her gullet. She'll be on special food for a while and once she's home, will have to be fed every few hours.'

'Goodness. Why didn't you let me know? You must have known how worried I was.'

'I felt so bad at blaming you. I wasn't sure how to apologise. I'm sorry.'

'At least I know it wasn't my fault. Goodness, poor Molly. Have you told your sister yet?'

'It's still the middle of the night . . . well, early in the morning there. I'm sorry again. I must get to bed now. I feel totally drained.'

'Thanks anyway. Night.' She put the

phone down and told Jeannie the latest news.

'So you didn't need to blame yourself. I'm glad she's all right, anyway. Why hadn't he let us know?'

'I think he was too ashamed for blaming me. Well, that was a nice little earner while it lasted. I suppose I'm now back to relying on party bookings.

'Speaking of which, I must get organised for Saturday. I'll have to let the mother know Molly won't be coming with us. Hope she still wants me to do the party or all the food I bought will be wasted.'

Fit for a Princess

It seemed a long night to Sarah-Louise. She was tossing and turning for most of it and finally fell asleep when it was nearly morning. Jeannie came to her door and woke her in time to get a lift to school.

She heard nothing more from Olly and knew the dog was staying at the vet's for at least the rest of today.

She stopped at the supermarket to do some shopping on her way back from dropping off Jeannie, making the most of having use of the car.

She was hoping to have it still the next day for the party. She had already phoned the mother of the party child and told her about Molly's illness and that she wouldn't be present. It was all approved.

She spent most of the day baking and preparing for the party. It actually seemed much easier without having to look after Molly and take her out regularly.

By the time she was due to go and collect Jeannie most things were done and ready to go. She just needed to make sandwiches the next morning.

She had even made a birthday cake and decorated it in true princess style with a little sparkly tiara perched on top for the little girl to wear.

She drove round to Jeannie's school and sat in the car park waiting for her friend. At last she appeared at the door and Sarah-Louise drove over to collect her.

'Sorry. Got delayed by the Head. She didn't like the fact I stayed in my classroom at lunchtime. Honestly, it was that or stay away for the rest of this week. That woman!'

'It's Friday. The weekend. You can have a good rest and maybe feel much better on Monday. Ready to go now?'

'Yes of course. I really don't want to see this place again for the next two days at least. You'd think she'd be grateful I made the effort, wouldn't you?

'Anyway, have you heard anything from Olly? How's Molly?'

'Nothing at all. I toyed with the idea of phoning the vet's but decided they probably wouldn't tell me anything. I then thought I'd ring Olly but decided against that, too. You'd think he'd have told me how she is, wouldn't you?'

'We could ring him when we get home.'

'I suppose. Oh, I don't know. I really liked him. In fact I thought he was going to be quite special until all this happened. He seemed so unreasonable about it and seemed to blame me for causing Molly's illness. And in fact it was all his sister's fault.'

'So tell him.'

'How on earth can I say anything to him?'

'Watch it!' Jeannie interrupted. 'There's a car trying to overtake.'

'Sorry. He's an idiot for trying it

there. Get lost,' she yelled at the chap, who could hear nothing she was saying.

'Calm down, love. I know you're probably hurting a bit but it isn't worth upsetting yourself. Olly's lovely but he's only one bloke.'

'Maybe.'

'But you've only known him for just over a week.'

'I know all that. But sometimes, you just know. I'm sure you know what I mean. Anyway, it really looks as if he's now in the past. And I need to find another job.

'I know it wasn't much I was getting from Molly minding but it was at least enough to keep me going.' She stopped in the car park and then realised she needed to drive closer for Jeannie to get out.

'It's OK. I can walk from here,' Jeannie told her.

'Really? If you're sure.'

'If you can carry my bag, I'll make it using the crutches. It'll be good for me.'

Sarah-Louise watched as she got out

of the car, adjusted the crutches and set off towards the flat. She was certainly greatly improved from a couple of days ago.

'Well done. You are getting better, even if it's only at managing the crutches.'

'I do feel more mobile anyway. It's good. Maybe I could even go shopping tomorrow.'

'You are joking? I was hoping to borrow your car for the party. How can you drive?'

'Oh, yes. I was thinking you might like to go with me. But of course, if you have a party . . . '

'Yes, I do. I've been cooking and preparing all day. Just got to do sandwiches and pack it all in the car tomorrow. Assuming I can still borrow your car.'

'I suppose you'll have to. Perhaps you should insure your own car again, if you're planning to do more business. Outside catering for parties and so on. After all, you're a pretty good cook.

Speaking of which . . . what are we having for supper?'

'Fish pie. It's all ready for heating when we want it.'

Unlike the previous weekend, it was a fairly relaxed evening with both girls watching television. No calls came from Olly and Sarah-Louise was doing her best to try to forget about him.

It wasn't really working, as he crept into her thoughts about every three minutes. It got to nine o'clock and she took a deep breath.

'I can't wait any longer. I've got to phone and see how Molly is. I can't believe he's just left us hanging and not even told us. What do you think?'

'I agree. Not very good at all. Go on then, call him.' Sarah-Louise nodded and dialled his number. He took ages to answer and she was about to hang up.

'Hello?'

'Hi. It's me. Sarah-Louise. I'm wondering how Molly is? Is she home yet?'

'She's coming home tomorrow. Sorry,

I suppose I should have called you.'

'Well, we were wondering. How are you?'

'I'm OK. Pretty stressed, actually. I emailed my sister to tell her the news and she was on the verge of flying back but I managed to persuade her there was nothing she could do.'

'Goodness. Pretty dramatic.'

'Typical of my sister. Look, I'm feeling very mixed up about all this. I really did blame you for letting her eat something but it turns out it wasn't your fault at all. I'm so sorry.'

'I knew it wasn't me. Don't worry about it.'

'It was pretty serious in the end. If she'd been left for another day or two it could have been fatal . . . Thankfully, the op went well and she should make a good recovery.'

'Thank goodness for that. So, panic over.'

'Looks like it.'

She paused for a moment, waiting for him to ask her to look after the dog again. He said nothing. She took the plunge.

'Will you want me to look after her again?'

'I'm not sure. Let me think about it. I'll call you tomorrow. She should be coming home then.'

'I do have a party tomorrow afternoon. You've probably forgotten with all the hoo-ha.'

'Oh, yes. I had forgotten. I'll call at some point anyway. Better go now.'

'Right. Bye then.'

'Bye.'

'That was pretty unsatisfactory,' she said when she put the phone down. 'He doesn't know whether he wants me to have Molly or not. He'd forgotten about the party tomorrow.'

'Well, he's been pretty worried for the past couple of days. I doubt he's even thought of us or what we're doing. Why should he? He's been phoning America and sorting out insurance and so on.'

'All right. I'll give him the benefit of

the doubt. I'll have to start looking for another job on Monday. Or Sunday even.'

'How about your idea of catering for adults? That might be a good idea. Get some cards done and scatter them around, especially at the kids' parties. I'm sure you'll do a good job there and probably parents will be impressed.'

'I'll give it some thought. Right, I've got to sort out my princess gear and get ready for tomorrow's big event.'

Still feeling a bit down, Sarah-Louise went into her room and took out her princess outfit. It was a bit grubby but she thought it would do. Perhaps she could sponge off the worst marks without washing the whole outfit. She took it into the kitchen and began splashing around.

'What ever are you doing?' Jeannie called.

'Cleaning up my princess togs. There's a mark in the middle of the skirt. Think I remember the dear little tyke who caused it. Oh, no! The colour's run. Now what am I going to do?'

'Make some more splashes of colour runs so it looks like a pattern. Or wear a pinny. Haven't you got a pretty apron?'

'I don't know. Honestly, this is the worst thing that could have happened. How on earth am I going to be a princess in a few hours if I don't have a dress? Besides, princesses don't wear aprons.'

'Unless it's part of the outfit. Bring it here and let me see.'

Sarah-Louise came through with her damaged dress. There was a large patch in the middle of the skirt which was paler than the rest and showed up very badly.

'Right, here's what we'll do,' Jeannie said calmly. 'I've got a long white frilly petticoat. If we split the dress up the middle and cut the patch out, I can then fit in my petticoat to look like a sort of double skirt layer.'

'But it's almost nine-thirty now. It'll

take for ever to repair,' Sarah-Louise wailed.

'Rubbish. You get the sewing machine out and I'll find my petticoat. Half an hour and it'll be as good as new. Find the scissors, too.'

Sarah-Louise did as she was told and waited for Jeannie to come back. She wasn't at all sure what Jeannie intended to do but there was no alternative.

Sarah-Louise watched in horror as her flatmate slashed down the front of the dress, chopping out the entire bleached stain. She then attached the frilly petticoat at the waist and stitched down the sides, folding the original material to make an overlap in a sort of Bo-Peep style.

'There you are. It's a bit crude but it'll do.'

'It's lovely. Thank you so much. You always were good with fabric and thank you for the petticoat. I'll buy you another one to make up.'

'Heavens, no. I haven't worn it for years. Glad I could make use of it.'

'You are amazing. Even managing to use the sewing machine with a sprained ankle. I'm hopeless at doing anything like that. Think I'd better get to bed now or I'll never be up in time tomorrow.'

'I'll go, too. Sleep well.'

Things Are Looking Up!

The party all went according to plan and the mother of the child was delighted.

'It was the easiest party I've ever had. Pity you can't do the same thing for adults.'

'I was planning to start an more adult version. Coming to people's homes and cooking for their dinner party in their own kitchens and then serving it.'

'Oh, that's a thought. I was more thinking of a party for my husband's work colleagues. Bits and pieces on sticks and so on. And wine, of course.'

'I could certainly do that. Presumably without the princess outfit!' They both laughed.

'Give me some idea of costs per head and We'll take it from there. Now, I'll write you a cheque for today.' She handed it over with thanks.

Sarah-Louise looked at it and gasped. She had been given an extra £50.

'Wow, thank you so much.'

'I'm very grateful to you.'

'I'll just load everything into the car and leave you in peace.' At this rate, Sarah-Louise was thinking, she could re-licence her own car and be independent. Life was certainly improving . . . at least her financial life was improving.

She parked and collected all her things she had packed in large plastic box. She staggered to the door of the flat with it all, still clad in her princess gear. A car stopped close by and out got Olly.

'Hi, there. I thought you might like to see the invalid. I've got her in the car.'

Sarah-Louise dumped the box on the ground and went over to look. There Molly sat, looking most accusingly at both of them.

She had a large sort of cone over her head and Sarah-Louise could see she was shorn of hair for quite a long way down her front.

'Oh, poor dog. You've really been through the mill, haven't you?'

Molly tried hard to look enthusiastic and wag her tail but it was all rather lost.

'What on earth are you dressed as?' Olly looked Sarah-Louise up and down with amusement.

'A princess, of course. I'm just on my way back from doing a party. Are you coming in?'

'If I can get Molly out of the car I will. If not, it's a case of love you and leave you.'

Wish you meant that, Sarah-Louise was thinking. Well, the first bit, at least. She felt her usual attraction to this man, despite the way she felt she'd been treated.

'I'll take this lot in and come back to help, if you need me.' She went inside and shouted to Jeannie that Olly was outside and on his way in.

'That's good. Is Molly with him?'

'Yes. I'm just going to grab my jeans and get out of this clobber. Won't be a minute.'

She did the fastest change ever and shot outside to see where Olly was. He was struggling with the huge dog who was half in and half out of his car. He couldn't get her to step forward and her rear seemed to be stuck in the doorway.

'Can I help somehow?' she asked.

'Perhaps if you got into the car on the other side, you could give her a push? If I'd known it would be this difficult, I wouldn't have tried. I'd just have gone straight home with her.'

'You mean you've only just collected her from the vet?'

He nodded as he was struggling.

'She got in there quite easily. Heavens, whatever am I going to do?'

'I'll give her a shove from the inside if you can give her a pull.'

'Tricky. I can't get hold of anything to pull on. I don't want to break the stitches.'

'Pushing from this end is like trying

to move a furry mountain. What on earth can we do?'

'I'll change places with you. Maybe I could push a bit harder or something. Her front paws are on the ground and I really don't know why she won't move further on.' They changed places and Molly continued to stand there, half in and half out of the car.

'Come on, you dopey dog. Come and see Jeannie. She'll be pleased to see you, you know. Come on, girl.' With an enormous heave from her rear, Molly moved out at last and stood and shook her enormous head.

'You know what? I think she doesn't like the lampshade thing round her head,' Sarah-Louise said. 'I really can't see how she could lick her wound if she didn't have it on.'

'Let's take her inside and we could try taking it off for a while,' Olly suggested.

They almost dragged the unwilling dog to the door of the flat, stopping on the grass to allow her the chance to relieve herself. It really was as if she was ashamed of the large collar round her neck, put there by the vet.

Olly stopped to take it off and she became a different dog. Her tail wagged and her head lifted with pleasure.

'Well done you,' Olly said. 'Well spotted. Whoever would have thought a dog could be so vain? She really didn't like wearing it, did she?'

'Probably it felt uncomfortable. Looking at the shape of her head, I'm sure she won't be able to reach her incision. She does look strange, shorn the way she is. Poor Molly.' Sarah-Louise opened the door and called out to her flatmate. 'Visitor for you, Jeannie.'

'Oh, Molly. How lovely to see you. Poor old thing. You'll feel cold. Doesn't she have to have one of those lampshade things?'

'She's too embarrassed to wear it,' Olly said. 'You should see the trouble we had getting her out of the car. Anyway, how are you getting on?'

'Much better, thanks. Back at work now though my Head is not grateful.'

'I'll put the kettle on, shall I?' Sarah-Louise offered, leaving the pair to chat. At least she felt they were now all talking again. She could put Olly's short temper down to his worries over his sister's dog. She made some coffee and took it in to the others.

'So it was all I could do to stop Emily from flying back here,' he was saying.

'Emily is your sister?' Sarah-Louise asked.

'Yes. She's older than me and very bossy. You should see the list of instructions she left for me to look after this dog. I didn't bother you with them before but maybe I'd better take more notice in future. She was devastated to discover it was more her fault than ours — her child's sock that did the damage.'

'At least I don't have any small socks lying around here. Does this mean you want me to look after Molly again?' Sarah-Louise asked.

'I'm actually taking this next week off as holiday so I can look after her myself. Hope that's OK with you?'

'Course. I don't have any particular plans. I want to work on my next venture as well. I'm going to start a 'cook in your own home' service. You know, dinner parties and such.

'If I cook in their own homes, I don't have to get approval from authorities or anybody. And I've been asked to do a sort of cocktail party'

'That sounds good. Well done.'

'I'm not sure about costing it, though. I don't want to charge too much but I do need to make it pay.'

'I'll help if I can. It's my sort of thing. I do this sort of stuff most days at work. You know, costing and profit and such.'

'That would be great. Thanks a lot. Mind you, I'm not quite reaching your standards.'

'Are we having any supper tonight?' Jeannie asked, sounding a bit plaintive.

Sarah-Louise felt slightly irritated. She'd been working all afternoon and would have loved Jeannie to have made just a little effort.

'I suppose I'd better look and see what there is. Omelettes or something?'

'I suppose so. Isn't there any meat or fish? I quite fancy something a bit more substantial than omelettes. How about you, Olly?'

'Well, I wasn't really inviting myself to supper. I could always go and fetch a takeaway.'

'Brilliant,' Jeannie said looking more enthusiastic than she had all day. 'I fancy a Chinese. How about the rest of you? Oh, and could you get extra prawn crackers? I adore them. And chicken chow mein. Must have that. Preferably with cashew nuts.'

'Sounds like you've already decided. Are you going to pay for it all?' Sarah-Louise snapped.

'It's OK. I'll buy it,' Olly said.

'No, you can't. You're always buying things for us and it's not fair.'

'Don't be silly. I don't mind. What's a few quid on a Chinese takeaway? Even with extra prawn crackers?'

'It's a lot to me. I don't earn much and still have loads of bills to pay.' Sarah-Louise was trying to be realistic and really felt Jeannie should offer to pay. After all, she was still earning reasonable money and wasn't spending much at the moment. She didn't offer, however.

'Don't worry. I'll go and get something. Hope you can manage Molly. She really needs to go out . . . not sure you'll be able to get her to move, though.'

'I'll try, don't worry. I can take her round the side where there's a patch of rough ground. Not too far for her to walk.'

Sarah-Louise wondered if she should say anything to Jeannie but decided against starting any more arguments.

She called to Molly to try and motivate her to go out but the dog seemed most unwilling to move.

Sarah-Louise stared at Molly and knelt down to look into her face. Her eyes looked very sad and almost pleading. She held out her hand to her but Molly simply laid her head down again with a deep sigh.

'You really are a poor old girl, aren't you?' she said softly. The dog tried to wag her tail but it was a pretty feeble attempt.

'I wonder if she's just getting over the anaesthetic or if there's some else wrong with her?' she said out loud.

'I don't know. Are you going to stay down there or get some plates warming ready for when Olly comes back?' Jeanette asked.

'I'm very concerned about the dog. Perhaps you could manage to put some plates in the oven? I'm going to try to get her outside.'

'I probably wouldn't be able to lift the plates. Surely it's not too much to ask you to do it?'

'How much have you moved off that sofa today?'

'Don't know what you mean,' Jeanette snapped.

'Doesn't look to me as if you've done anything. Not good for you.'

'You have no idea how painful it is. Every time I stand up the blood rushes down and it really hurts.'

'Oh dear, poor old you.' Sarah-Louise couldn't keep the sarcasm out of her words. She went back to trying to coax Molly and ignored Jeannie's grunts and moans as she got up from the sofa.

Sarah-Louise watched her limping so heavily towards the kitchen and gave a cynical smile. She really could move better than that but clearly was milking the situation.

There was a crash from the kitchen and a string of curses. Sarah-Louise stayed where she was and continued to pet the dog.

'Plates are in the oven,' Jeannie said grumpily.

'Well done.' Sarah-Louise waited for her to say something about the crash but nothing came. She gave up on the dog and rose and sat down again.

Almost an hour later, she remarked that Olly was taking a long time.

'It is a Saturday night and there's probably a queue.'

'Maybe. Wonder where he's gone for it?'

'No idea.' They sat waiting for a while longer and Sarah-Louise began to worry.

'I'm going to phone his mobile. He may be stuck in traffic or his car's broken down.' She dialled his number but there was a message to say the number was not available. 'Strange. Perhaps he's in a typical Cornish black spot.'

'What did it say?'

'Number not available. It wasn't the usual leave a message or anything. Oh well. I suppose we just have to wait.'

Jeannie put the television on and they watched some drivel for a while. It was almost nine o'clock and there was still no sign of Olly.

'Do you think he's had an accident?' Sarah-Louise said at last.

'I'd doubt it. I don't think there's anything we can do. I'm absolutely starving. Should we have something to eat? I'm beginning to feel a bit light-headed.'

'OK. I'll do an omelette, then if he does turn up, at least you can eat whatever he brings.'

'Thanks, love. That would be good.'

Sarah-Louise went into the kitchen and worked on the omelette. It only took a few minutes and she took it in to her friend.

'Delicious. Aren't you having one?'

'Nah. I'm getting really worried now. Do you think I should phone the hospital?'

'Course not. How on earth would he feel to know you'd done that?'

'Oh, I don't know. If he had an accident, nobody would know about us. They wouldn't even let us know, would they?

'And Molly needs feeding too. Olly had only just collected her from the vet's. I wonder if she'd eat tuna? I've got a tin of that in the cupboard. If I mix it with something. I might try it.'

'She's a dog, not a cat. Do dogs eat fish?'

'I don't know. But she must be starving. It's ages since she could have eaten. I'll see what else there is in the cupboard.'

She was delighted to find a can of corned beef. That would certainly fit the bill. She opened it and mixed some slightly stale crackers into it and took it into the lounge. 'Here you are, Molly. A positive feast for you.' Her head rose and she sniffed. Then she staggered to her feet and began to eat. It didn't take long and then she wagged her tail and moved towards the door.

'She probably wants to go out now,' Sarah-Louise said. 'I'll take my phone with me in case he rings.'

Molly performed as good dogs should and was ready to go back inside.

'Any news?' Sarah-Louise asked Jeannie on her return.

'Nothing at all,' Jeannie replied.

The Awful Truth

Jeannie was yawning. It was after half-past ten.

'Sorry,' she murmured. 'I feel totally shattered. Do you mind if I go to bed?'

'You go and get some sleep. I'll stay here and maybe lie on the sofa. I don't feel I can leave Molly and well, I want to wait and see if there's a call. I really can't think what's happened to him. I've tried his number again but got the same message.'

'I feel mean leaving you.'

'Don't worry. No point in both is us staying around.'

'Well, he is your boyfriend.'

'Is he? I just thought he was a friend of both of us. He seems keen enough on you.'

'What on earth do you mean?'

'Oh, nothing. Just me being silly, I expect. Go on. Get off to bed. I'll take over your sofa surfing.'

Jeannie went off and got into bed. She did feel bad about leaving her flatmate but she did feel very weary. She was soon fast asleep.

Sarah-Louise on the other hand, was lying worrying. Olly must have had an accident. There was no way he'd have just driven off and left them with the dog. Something really bad must have happened or he'd have called.

By two o'clock, she really couldn't face her thoughts any longer and called the police. She spoke quietly, so she didn't disturb Jeannie.

'Has there been a road traffic accident in the town this evening? Only my friend went to get a takeaway and he hasn't come back.'

'What is the name of your friend?'

'Olly Jones. Oliver, I suppose.'

'And your name, madam?'

'Sarah-Louise Jamieson.'

'One moment, please.' He was quiet for several moments and she began to get worried. Then the officer spoke again. 'Are you a relative of Mr Jones?'

'No. Just a close friend.'

'Then I'm sorry but I don't have any information for you.'

'But I've got his dog here, with me. Is he hurt or what? He isn't . . . ?'

'Just a moment, madam.'

'Please don't do this to me. I love him. Please, put me out of my misery. Is he dead?'

'He's been attacked. I'm sorry but I don't have much information. You could go to the hospital and see how he is there.'

'Attacked? How do you mean?'

'He was assaulted outside Park Royal Chinese takeaway. A gang of youths were the perpetrators.'

'But how is he? Please can you tell me?'

'Go to the hospital. They'll tell you.'

'OK. I'll go right away.' She put the phone down, scribbled a note to Jeannie and set off in Jeannie's car. It was about three o'clock and she was positively shaking. She drove carefully, not wanting to risk any more accidents. She parked and ran into the casualty department.

'Please, do you have Olly Jones in here? He was apparently assaulted this evening.'

'Are you a relative, madam?'

'I'm his fiancée,' she lied. She wasn't about to be put off again.

'Just a moment. I'll see if I can find out how he is. Take a seat for a moment.' Sarah-Louise was indicated a row of chairs where patients could wait. She went and sat down, finding herself shivering slightly despite the heat in the hospital. The nurse returned with a doctor in tow.

'The doctor will help you.'

They nodded to each other.

'I'm afraid he's still unconscious.'

'Can you tell me what happened? The police said I should come here to find out.'

'He was attacked outside the take-away place. Punched and kicked around the head. He was carrying some food and that was snatched.'

'You mean to say, he was beaten up for the sake of food?'

'Not really. Well, I don't think so. I believe the youths were high on something or other but don't quote me on that. I think the police took them — or some of them — into custody.'

'This is terrible. Will he be all right?'

'We're hoping so. We'll have to wait till he comes round and possibly then, he'll be put into an induced coma. To give him recovery time, you understand.'

'You're implying he might have brain damage?'

'It is possible. But we won't know for a while.'

'Can I see him?'

'Not much point. I'd suggest you go home and get some rest and come back later in the morning.'

'Please. Can't I just look in on him? I won't speak to him or anything.'

'Well, all right. You can just go into the room and look at him. He's still unconscious, don't forget, so there won't be any response.'

'It's so awful. I can hardly believe it happened so quickly.' She was talking to the doctor, as they walked along the corridor. 'One usually thinks Truro is so safe.'

'It usually is, until there's some lunatic around who can't control himself. He's in here.'

The doctor opened the door and she moved in towards the bed. She could scarcely believe what she was seeing. Olly looked terrible with bruises on his face and a load of machines buzzing away, keeping his alive, she supposed.

'Oh my goodness. Do you think he'll get better? He looks so awful,' Sarah-Louise said.

'I did warn you. Normally we don't let close relatives in to see patients at this stage. Actually, you could help with details about his parents. Speak to the nurse in the department and give her the details.'

Sarah-Louise swallowed hard. She

had no idea where they lived or even if there were any parents around.

She knew he had a sister in America but had no idea of her address or where she was staying.

'His sister is in America at the moment. We're looking after her dog but I don't know where she's staying and well, I don't even know about his parents.' She felt dreadful about it. How on earth could she be his fiancée and not know if he even had any parents?

'Erm . . . right. I'll see the nurse.'

'OK. And don't worry. My gut feeling is that he'll recover and all will be well.'

'Thanks, doctor.' She went across to nurses' station and spoke to the nurse, hopefully trying to avoid saying why she knew so little about Olly. She felt quite stupid when the nurse asked her for details.

She knew his sister was called Emily and thought she was married but had no idea of where she lived. She didn't know if his parents were still alive, either. Apart from knowing his name and address, that was pretty much it. The nurse stared at her.

'And you say you're engaged to this man?'

'Well, no, not really. But we are pretty close. I'm looking after his dog. Or rather, his sister's dog. She's lovely. The dog, I mean.'

'I suggest you go home now and get some rest. You can phone in the morning to see how he is.'

'Right. I'll do that. Thanks.' Sarah-Louise left the hospital and looked at her watch. It was now almost four o'clock. Hardly worth going to bed, she thought.

She hoped Molly would be all right. She didn't even have her blanket or bed or anything else.

She would need to go shopping early the next day to buy dog food and anything else the dog would need. What a mess.

She wondered if Olly had told his sister where she lived or even passed on her phone number. She should have taken his phone and then she would at least have had his list of people. Perhaps she could get it the next day, if they'd let her.

Back at home, Molly was lying stretched out in the main room.

'You do take up a lot of room, don't you, girl?' She spoke kindly to the large dog. Molly lifted her head and wagged her tail rather feebly.

'Aren't you feeling too good?' Sarah-Louise said anxiously. 'Do you want to go out? Come on, then. We can go outside and you will feel better after that.'

She tried to encourage Molly to get up and then took her to the door. It was hard work persuading her to go outside but eventually she managed it. Molly gave a loud grunt and did as she was told.

'Good girl.' Sarah-Louise took her back inside and settled her down again before she went to bed herself.

To her surprise, Sarah-Louise slept

very well. She woke at almost nine o'clock to find Jeannie standing by her bed with a cup of coffee.

'Sorry, didn't mean to wake you. How did you get on?'

'Oh, goodness. What time is it?'

'Just after nine. How was Ollie?'

Sarah-Louise gave her a brief run-down on what had happened.

'He's still unconscious. They kept him under to give him time to heal a bit. I looked in on him but didn't speak or anything.'

'You were lucky they let you in.'

'I said we were engaged. They didn't argue but then I rather let the side down by knowing nothing at all about his family. Stupid, really, but I didn't even know if he has parents still living.'

'Yes, he does. They live in Spain somewhere.'

'How do you know that?'

'He mentioned it once. I just remembered. His sister is in Illinois. A small town near Chicago.'

'Goodness. You should have gone to

the hospital. At least you'd have seemed more credible than I did. I must phone the hospital and see how he is today.'

Sarah-Louise rose and pulled on her jeans and a shirt and made her phone call. A few minutes later she put the phone down.

'Well, it seems he's still asleep. Unconscious, that is. I'm going to take Molly out for a walk and then I'll go to the hospital again. Is that all right with you? I mean, can I borrow the car . . . your car again?'

Jeannie's expression flickered for a moment.

'Yes, of course. I'll stay here with Molly. Have we got anything to feed her?'

'I'll get some food. What do you think she eats?'

'Dunno. Dog food, I suppose. Biscuits? Tinned stuff?'

'OK. I'll get a few cans and some biscuits. She's supposed to have some special food. I think she's only fed twice a day. Come on then, Molly. Let's go.'

The two of them set out from the flat and walked slowly a little way. Molly looked longingly back towards the way they had come.

'Do you want to go back?' Sarah-Louise asked the dog. Molly wagged her tail and turned round. 'OK. That will do for now. I'll go and get you some food and you can have a nice breakfast. How do you feel about that?'

'I beg your pardon?' an elderly gentleman said as he walked past them.

'Sorry, I was talking to the dog.'

'She's a lovely dog. What sort is she?'

'A Newfoundland. She's a bit delicate after having surgery.'

'I wondered about her strange collar. Thought she may be fierce or something. Well, thank you for the information. I now know what a Newfoundland looks like. Good morning.' He touched his cap as he walked away.

Sarah-Louise smiled, thinking it was nice to meet a friendly face. She took the dog home and left her there while she went to buy food for her. Her own tummy rumbled and she realised she hadn't eaten since . . . well, she couldn't remember.

Was it too early for a pasty, she wondered. They were baking them in a shop she passed and she went in and bought herself one.

She collected dog food and went back to the car where she sat and ate the pasty very quickly. That felt better. Perhaps she should have bought another one for Jeannie but she hadn't so she'd stay silent about her feast.

When she got back, her flatmate was in the kitchen, looking somewhat pained.

'I was trying to make some toast but it's very difficult with my ankle being so painful.'

'Perhaps you should go and have it x-rayed. I would have thought it should be much better after over a week.'

'I'm not pretending, you know. It really is very painful.'

'I'm sure it is. I was just thinking it

should be less painful and wondering if you had a mis-diagnosis. I'm not criticising.'

'Perhaps it is a bit better,' Jeannie murmured. 'Perhaps I should try driving again.'

Sarah-Louise cursed silently. It was going to be very difficult to visit the hospital without a car and her own vehicle was sitting in the car park without any tax or insurance.

'I was going to go to the hospital after I've fed Molly. Do you want to come with me? You could try driving then.'

'I might. I'll see after we've had some toast. Can you do it, please, love?'

'OK. I'll feed Molly first. She must be very hungry by now.'

'So am I,' Jeannie said. 'I'm starving. Well, I did have a sandwich. I managed to do that balancing on one leg.'

'There you go, Molly. Eat up and hope I got the right food for you.' She watched as the large dog heaved herself up and started to eat. Within seconds her bowl was empty. 'Goodness. Should I give her some more, do you think?'

'Dunno. Maybe not. Maybe you could give her some more later on.'

'I'll make some toast now and coffee. I really need some coffee. Some decent coffee. Then I must get off. Oh, you need to decide if you're coming too.'

'I'm not sure I feel up to it. Perhaps I'll stay at home and rest.'

'Do you want an egg with your toast?' Sarah-Louise called from the kitchen.

'Please. That would be lovely.'

She put the coffee pot on and made the toast and poached a couple of eggs. She did feel slightly guilty about her illicit pasty but what the heck? Surely it was up to Jeannie to feed herself if she was hungry.

She carried the tray through and set the simple meal on the table. Jeannie made no movement towards the table so Sarah-Louise thrust the tray towards her. She really was making a meal out of being unwell, she thought. Molly had settled down again and looked up at them both pleadingly.

'What is it, girl?' Sarah-Louise asked. 'Are you missing your owner?' The dog wagged her tail and looked hopeful. 'I'm afraid you'll have to make do with us for a while longer.'

Sarah-Louise ate her breakfast, drank the coffee and stood up.

'I'm off now. Sure you don't want to come?'

'I would like to but don't really feel able. Not this morning.'

'OK. Don't know what time I'll be back.'

'Will you get something organised for lunch? Only I won't be able to go out at all, especially if I'm dog-sitting, and you'll have the car anyway.'

'I will get mine back on the road very soon, I promise. Bye, then.'

'Bye. Give Olly my love.'

'Sure thing, assuming he's conscious again.'

She set off for the hospital. At least the traffic was reasonably quiet, being a

Sunday morning. She even found space in the car park nearest the hospital, which surprised her. It was usually a case of driving for what seemed like miles to find somewhere to stop.

She went inside and asked at the desk if there was any news about Olly's current location. Armed with the correct knowledge, she set off along the corridor. She did stop at the nurses' station to ask after him.

'He's recovered consciousness and doesn't seem to have any brain damage. Keeping him under yesterday was the best thing and I'm pleased to say, it worked.'

'Can I see him, then?'

'He is a bit sleepy still but yes, you can go in. Don't try to wake him or engage him in too much conversation.'

'Right. Promise I won't. I can't wait to see him.'

Bad to Worse

Sarah-Louise walked towards Olly's room with some trepidation, unsure of how he would be. She had told them she was his fiancée — a blatant lie but she had wanted to be sure to see him and find out what had happened. Hospitals were notoriously difficult with anyone who wasn't a relation.

She entered his room quietly and stood beside the bed, looking at him. His poor face was bruised and he looked generally pretty battered. His eyes were closed but he was breathing steadily. He did look much better than the previous evening. He stirred as if aware she was there.

'Jeannie? Jeannie, is that you? Are you there?'

Jeannie? Jeannie? Sarah-Louise heard, unable to believe what she was hearing.

'It's Sarah-Louise. You know, Sarah-Louise who is looking after your dog, or rather your sister's dog.'

'Oh, Jeannie, please say it's you.'

The wretched man, she was thinking. He must be in love with her flatmate. Really, that was too much to comprehend. Whenever had he spent time with Jeannie?

'No, it isn't Jeannie. It's Sarah-Louise. Her flatmate.' She spoke angrily and sharply, forgetting how ill he was. His eyes opened and he looked at her.

'Sarah-Louise. How nice of you to come to see me. I'm sorry about the meal.'

'You can actually remember what happened? I mean about the food you were buying — and us and everything?'

'Course I do. Why wouldn't I?'

'What about the guys who came at you and beat you up?'

'Well, no, I don't remember too much about that. I probably fainted or something but I do remember seeing them.

'I made the stupid mistake of fighting back. I should have just let them take the food. I felt a punch in my face and that was it. I think it was a good thing I'm a craven coward. I just lay on the ground and waited for it all to stop.'

'Goodness me. I think you were pretty brave, actually. Anyway, how are you feeling now?'

'Bit battered but nothing too awful. I say, I suppose you couldn't get me a toothbrush and toothpaste, could you? They've given me a sponge off, largely to remove the blood, but my teeth feel like they could do with a good clean.'

'I'll go to the shop. I'm sure they'll sell things like that. Won't be long.'

She went along the corridors to the shop. She picked up a toothbrush and toothpaste and also a magazine. She didn't have a lot of cash with her so was limited.

What on earth did he mean about asking for Jeannie? She felt angry and not a little frustrated. Heavens, she had always been the one to do socialising and she had introduced him to their house.

She had often suspected he was getting friendly with Jeannie and now it seemed to have happened. She paid for her purchases and went back to his ward.

'Sarah-Louise. Thank you so much. You are good to me.' He held out his hand, attached to his pulse monitor. She took his hand and smiled.

'Not at all. You've been good to us. I'll tell Jeannie you asked for her.' She couldn't stop herself saying that and then bit her lip, knowing she was being bitchy.

'Jeannie? So how is she?'

'Fine. She's staying home to mind Molly.'

'Oh, my goodness. What about food? I must give you some money to buy her meat. Oh, dear, sorry — they took my wallet. I will recompense you eventually, I promise.'

'We got Molly some cans this morning and biscuits. I had no idea what you feed her on or indeed how much to give her.'

'Hopefully, it will only be for today and I should be home by tomorrow at the latest.'

Did you have credit cards in your wallet?'

'Yes. I suppose I should cancel them.'

'You certainly should. Bank cards and credit cards . . . the lot. It'll mean you have a wait for some new ones but better safe than sorry.'

'Those youths have caused so much trouble! I don't even have my phone. Heaven knows what damage they could do with that.'

'Right. We'll make a start with your phone. There's a bit of credit left on mine. Use that to tell your phone company what's happened. Come on.' She produced her phone from her bag and he took it gratefully.

'At least it's the same network.' He dialled a number and then started speaking, explaining what had happened to him. She looked at him from the other side of the room.

He did look a mess with bruises now coming out around his face. He seemed to be having some difficulty with breathing too, which was indicative of his rib injuries. Poor chap, she was thinking.

'Thanks very much. Bye,' he said into the phone. 'It seems that several calls have been made already but they will reimburse me for them and have cut off the phone so they can't make any more.

'I'll have to buy another phone I suppose and take out a new contract. All the hassle of letting people know my new number and . . . oh dear. It's all too much.' He flopped back against his pillows.

'Perhaps I could cancel your cards for you? I can look at the computer when I go home.'

'I don't think they'd allow that. All the passwords and stuff. I really need my laptop to be able to do it. Perhaps you could get it for me? It's back at home. Would you mind?'

'Not at all — but have you got some keys?'

'Oh, no! I've just realised they took them as well. I don't think my address is anywhere . . . oh yes, it's on my driving licence, isn't it? This just gets worse and worse. It was in my wallet and they took that.'

'The police will be here soon to interview you. You must tell them. Or perhaps you'd like to call them and tell them your problems? Or I will.'

'That would be good. If you don't mind. I feel exhausted now.'

Sarah-Louise nodded and went out of his room to call the police. Different officers were on duty so she had to explain the problems from scratch.

'Oh, yes, I believe I remember seeing that report. Hang on there and I'll take a look.'

'I'm on a mobile and don't have much credit left so be quick, please.'

'Give me your number and I'll call you back.' She did so then wandered along the corridor a little way, not wanting to be too far from Olly's room.

A nurse came along and asked if she needed help. She said she was waiting for a phone call, at which point her phone rang. The nurse nodded and went on her way.

'Right, I've now caught up on the case. Our patrol will go round to his house and check to see it's safe. We should get a locksmith to change to locks. We can organise that for you. What is his address?'

'I'll have to go and ask him. To get it exact, you understand.' She was still playing the part of his fiancée. 'Olly, what is your exact address? The police are on the phone and suggesting they go round to look, to make sure all is well.' He told her the address and she repeated it to the policeman.

'If you could be there too, it might be helpful. Unless Mr Jones could be there.'

'I'm sorry but he's still in hospital. And I don't really know his house at all.'

'We'll go and check it out anyway. I'm sure we shall see if there's been a break-in. Mind you, if they have the keys . . . '

'I'll come round and take a look.' They finished the conversation and she switched her phone off. 'It seems they want me to go round to the house. Is that OK?'

'Course. As long as you don't mind. It's very messy. You might remember I'd only just collected Molly from the vets. Oh goodness, will she be all right with Jeannie?'

'I'll pop back home first and check on them. At least Jeannie is more mobile now.'

'There's my car as well. Where do you think that is now? Oh, I could murder those kids. I just hope I can get out of here soon.'

Sarah-Louise left him and went home. She cursed the car parking authorities that she had to pay a large sum of money to even get her car out of the car-park. She drove back to the flat and let herself in.

'Oh, there you are,' Jeannie said rather grumpily. 'Thought you'd got lost.'

'I've got to go to Olly's place. Evidently they took his keys and his wallet so they have his address on his driving licence. Will you be all right to look after Molly?'

'Not much choice, is there? If you could let her out that would be helpful. And what about lunch? I could certainly do with something.'

'I'll call at the supermarket on my way back. We haven't got much in. There's always toast if you think you might be starving.'

'Great. Buy some pasties or something reasonably substantial. I assume you'll be taking my car?'

Sarah-Louise felt somewhat put upon but she rushed out with Molly and once she had her necessary walk, Sarah-Louise took her back inside.

She called out goodbye and set out for Porthcullion. At least she knew her way there having visited it for the party recently. Goodness, children's parties seemed a long way away. Was it really only yesterday that she was doing one? Seemed like a century ago.

Caught Red-handed

Porthcullion was peaceful at this time of day with most people eating lunch or gardening. It was a nice village, Sarah-Louise was thinking. Most of the houses were fairly large and the smaller places were all neat and tidy.

She drove down the road until she came the cul-de-sac where she knew Olly's house to be. There was a police car parked outside and two constables were walking round the outside.

'Good morning. You are?'

'Sarah-Louise Jamieson. I'm a friend of Olly's . . . the owner of the house.'

'Fine. All looks pretty quiet,' one of them said. 'Can you tell if anything's been disturbed inside?' She peered in through the window and decided it looked as she'd expected.

'I think it's all OK. Wait a moment . . . there's someone in there. I thought

I just saw a door closing . . . well, being pulled to. I'm sure of it.'

'And there isn't anyone you'd know might be there?'

'Not at all.'

The policeman started banging on the door but it seemed ineffectual.

'Come on. Open up or we'll break in.'

The second officer went round to the rear of the property and gave a sudden yell as someone rushed out.

They all ran round to see what was going on. Two young men were running away over the rear fence and into the fields behind the house.

The two policemen leaped over the fence and gave chase. They were obviously fitter than the two youths and soon caught up with them. They brought them back with handcuffs attached.

Both of the robbers seemed well out of it and were laughing as they slumped across the two policemen.

'Goodness, well done!' Sarah-Louise exclaimed.

'I'll just call the station and get someone to collect these two. Obviously they are part of the group who attacked your friend.'

'At least they've been caught. Do you think they are still taking drugs?'

'I think we'll find evidence of something in the house.

The policemen's colleagues arrived and the youths were escorted away to the waiting car which set off for the police station.

'Right, Sam,' one of the original constables said. 'Come on, let's go inside and we'll see what we can find.'

Sarah-Louise was interested to see around his house until she realised what a mess the two youths had made. She knew he would never have left it like this, with dirty pots in the sink and a frying pan full of grease. What on earth had they been doing?

Upstairs, the bed had been pulled around and drawers had been emptied all over the floor. She could hardly believe it all.

'It's awful what they've done to the place. They must have been in some sort of frenzy.'

'It's the drugs, I'm afraid. They didn't know what they were doing. They'd obviously spent the money they stole on fresh supplies. I've found some evidence of their apparatus in the front room.

'I don't think changing the locks will be necessary. They obviously came here soon after the robbery and their accomplices are already in custody. Pretty low chance they had time to get keys cut. We have got two of them still at the station.

'Now, if you'd like to leave us to it, I'll get something moving with forensics.'

'Can't I have a key? There's his car left somewhere, too. I'm sure all Olly's keys would be on one bunch.'

'Ah, yes, the car. What sort is it?'

'A red one.'

'And the make?'

'Erm . . . not sure. A Ford or Vauxhall?'

'I'm afraid it may have been crashed. We had a report of a car of that description found abandoned near here. Those crazed kids must have driven it back here and managed to drive into a wall.

'Must have been parked outside the takeaway place. I should think that must be the right car.'

'Oh, dear. Poor Olly. Seems that everything that could go wrong is going wrong.'

'I think perhaps you should go and see him and break the bad news to him, if he's well enough. I assume he can stay at your place?'

'Course. I'll take one of the keys anyway.'

Half an hour later, she was parking at the hospital again. How much was it going to cost her this time, she wondered. When she arrived at the ward, she found Olly sitting in a chair, fully dressed again.

His clothes were partially ripped and very grubby. Traces of blood were also present. She stared at his rather battered face and it looked as if he was going to have a really black eye.

'Glad you came back. I can go home in a few minutes. The nurse is organising some medication for me and was going to call you. Is that all right?'

'Course it is. But you really can't go home right away. You can come back to our place. The police are busy at your home and will be there for some time.'

'I see. And my car? I left it outside the takeaway place.'

'I'm so sorry but they took that and drove it back to your place — only they didn't quite make it.'

'What do you mean?'

'They drove into a wall. They were so high on something or other. You need to leave it to the police to sort out the worst of the mess.'

'How do you mean? Rest of the mess?'

'I'm afraid they spent the night at your house. I'll go back later and try to clean up a bit but for now, we'll get you back to our place and you can stay with Jeannie and Molly.

'Oh, heavens, I completely forgot. I was supposed to be buying provisions and something for lunch.'

'Bit late for lunch now, isn't it? Must be about three o'clock.'

'How much longer do you think you'll be? I could go to the supermarket and come back for you.'

'I shouldn't be too long. The nurse went off ages ago.'

'I'll go and see if I can find someone.' She left him and was just about to tackle the group at the nurse's station when Olly's nurse came rushing back.

'Sorry to keep you. Took ages to get them to dispense the drugs. They said there was a backlog and you didn't have priority. But here are your meds.'

'Presumably we can now go?' Olly asked.

'Yes indeed.' The nurse nodded. 'You have your outpatient's appointment, haven't you?'

'Yes, thanks. Thank you for looking after me.'

'You're very welcome. I hope you and your fiancée will be happy in the future.'

'My fiancée? Oh, I see. Yes, well I hope it works out.'

Sarah-Louise was blushing furiously and tried to cover her stupid pretence from earlier by laughing it off. As soon as they were clear of the ward, she turned to Olly and apologised.

'I'm sorry. But it was the only way I could get in to see you last night. They kept asking me things I couldn't answer and that made me realise how little I know about you. I don't even know if you have parents alive . . . '

'I do and they live in Spain. Have done for years.'

'I gathered you told Jeannie. Do you think they should be told about this attack?'

'Doubt they'd be interested. I rarely speak to them. They've made lives of their own in the sun and they don't really keep up with their kids.'

They reached Jeannie's car and she groped in her purse for enough change for the parking fee. She could just manage it.

'Sorry, I don't have any money at all. They cleared me out.' Olly grimaced.

'It's OK. I've got enough.' She went back to the machine and fed in her money.

'If you don't mind staying in the car, I'll just dash into Sainsbury's and get some food. Promise I won't be long.'

The shop was fairly full but she dashed round as fast as she could manage and tossed all manner of food into the trolley.

Dog food, Sarah-Louise reminded herself, and grabbed some cans and biscuits. She saw the smallest queue and dashed into it and started unloading.

Soon Sarah-Louise was back at the car and loaded the bags into the boot.

'Thank goodness for credit cards,' she murmured, as she got in. 'I just hope Jeannie will be all right. She's annoyed that I'm using her car all the time.'

'But if she can't drive anyway, what does it matter?'

* * *

'I wondered what on earth had happened to you,' Jeannie grumbled as she walked in. 'You left me for so long, I nearly called the police to see if you'd had an accident.'

'Sorry. I had to go to Olly's house with the police and then we had to wait for his medication at the hospital. Then of course I had to do the shopping.'

'I just hope you've got something to eat immediately. I'm dying of hunger here.' Jeannie was unimpressed by her flatmate's busy morning.

'I've got pasties for us all. I'd better take Molly out before I eat mine. Has she been all right?'

'She has got up a few times and

wandered round. Obviously I couldn't take her out.'

'Obviously not,' Sarah-Louise said with a slightly sarcastic tone. 'I'll put out your pasties and you two can eat them and then I'll get mine later.'

'I'm sorry. I should be taking Molly out.' Olly was sitting stroking the dog and petting her. She rolled on to her back.

Sarah-Louise handed the two of them their pasties and attached Molly's lead to her collar. When Sarah-Louise returned she unpacked the shopping and finally sat down to eat her pasty.

'Goodness, I could easily eat that all over again,' she remarked.

'Hope you got something nice for supper. Perhaps we can have it a bit earlier than usual,' Jeannie said.

'I got some chicken. Thought we'd have a casserole or something. We have to decide where Olly's going to sleep. He obviously can't go home tonight. His house needs cleaning and there's some washing that needs doing.'

'I could go back. It's a bit much for you to let me stay here. And there's Molly to consider as well.'

'Don't be silly,' Jeannie said. 'Of course you must stay. He can have your bed, can't he, Sarah-Louise? You can sleep on the sofa and Molly will probably be all right on the floor nearby. I've got to go to work tomorrow anyway so you'll have to drive me.'

Sarah-Louise refrained from making the sarcastic comment that immediately sprang to mind and turned away. Really, Jeannie was becoming impossible.

'I hope you'll soon be able to drive again,' was her only comment.

'Don't forget I've got a badly sprained ankle. I don't know how you think I can possibly drive again. You seem to have taken to using my car all the time anyway.'

Sarah-Louise refrained from pointing out that Jeannie had actually said earlier in the day that she thought she was ready to drive again.

'I'm going to get mine taxed and insured soon,' Sarah-Louise said. 'Now I've actually got some cash. I said as much to Olly, didn't I?'

'You did,' Olly confirmed. 'Look, I'll be fine on the sofa for tonight and maybe go back home tomorrow. That is, assuming you won't mind taking me.'

'Course not. I'll stay and help you to clear up the mess too.'

'That sounds typical. You can help him but seem to resent helping me. How long have you known him? Five minutes at least. Strikes me anything in trousers with a pulse and you're snapping after him like crazy.'

Jeannie sat there looking positively venomous. Sarah-Louise was totally nonplussed and sat with her mouth open. Olly looked desperately uncomfortable.

'Well, what do you have to say to that?' Jeannie demanded.

'Nothing,' Sarah-Louise replied. 'There's nothing I can say. I'd have thought I've been looking after you pretty well and went to help Olly in his hour of need.'

'You could take me home this evening. I'm sure I can manage,' Olly said in somewhat hurt tones.

'Not at all. There's too much to do at your place before you can stay there. Don't forget I've seen it.

'It's much too late for us to go there now. I'm going to make a start on supper. I'm sure we're all going to be ready for it when it's done.'

She went into the kitchen and started on the chicken. She felt tears burning and was struggling to suppress her anger. She wasn't sure she would ever forgive Jeannie for those words. Heavens, she had been feeling jealous of her flatmate at one point but now . . .

Well, perhaps she had been giving Olly more attention than usual but surely that was because he needed help. She certainly didn't feel as if she'd been hounding after him as

Jeannie had suggested.

She heard a movement behind her and turned. Olly was standing there, clutching himself round the ribs.

'I'm so sorry your friend has reacted like that,' he said. 'Thank you for all your help. I do appreciate it.

'After tomorrow, if you can take us back home, I think you should spent time with Jeannie. I don't like to think of me breaking up a beautiful friendship.'

'I don't think you have. Jeannie did that all by herself. Strange but I've never known her like this before.'

'I'll talk about it tomorrow. Can I help with anything?'

'Course not. You go and rest. Not much to do here anyway. Leave me to fester a bit. Once I'm over it, I'll be fine.'

'Perhaps I could take Molly out. That will save you one job.'

'Don't hurt yourself any more.'

He smiled and touched her shoulder. She felt a pulse of something like electricity where his fingers had been. Goodness, she thought, I'm really getting sensitive. She heard him calling out to Molly and then the door clicked shut.

She flung the chicken pieces into a casserole and added a few herbs and some stock. She put it in the oven along with some jacket potatoes. There was also some broccoli which she planned to cook at the last minute.

She went back into the other room and saw Jeannie was engrossed in a book. She sat down thinking she felt exhausted both physically and emotionally.

She closed her eyes and was almost nodding off when Olly arrived back at the door. She let him in and asked if he was all right.

'Fine. Think it did me good.'

'OK if I put the television on?' Sarah-Louise asked the others.

'Please yourself. You usually do anyway,' Jeannie sneered.

Sarah-Louise closed her eyes for a

moment, resisting the urge to retaliate. How would they ever come back from this? Only by her agreeing never to see Olly again and she certainly wasn't going down that route.

She put the television on and they watched a nature programme. None of them really took much in but it prevented more nasty comments.

When it was over she rose and went into the kitchen again.

She got on with the meal preparation and once it was nearly done, she took the cutlery through to lay the table.

Olly smiled at her and Jeannie scowled. She ignored both of them and went back to the kitchen.

'Gosh, this looks good,' Olly said appreciatively. 'Well done you.'

Once she had eaten Jeannie announced she was going to bed.

Once Jeannie had gone through to her bedroom, Sarah-Louise breathed a sigh of relief.

'I'm so sorry you had to witness that argument,' she said to Olly. 'I can't think why she was so spiteful.'

'I'll tell you why. She's just plain jealous. She asked me to . . . well . . . to go out with her and I said no. I said I was with you. Well, I am, aren't I?'

'Are you? I don't know.'

'She got a bit nasty with me when I told her I wasn't interested.'

'When was all this?'

'A few days ago. Before all the Molly trauma and before my accident.'

'Goodness me. I wonder why it's suddenly hit her like this. I mean, it's taken a few days, hasn't it?'

'Perhaps it's because she was left for so long today. She felt neglected.'

'I think she's putting it on a bit. She only has a sprain, for goodness' sake, and I think if she really tried she could easily drive herself.

'Still, if she did that, I'd be without a car so I won't say anything till my car's back on the road. I'd better go and clear up the kitchen mess.'

'I'll come and help.'

'There's no need. Really.'

'I'll come and talk to you anyway. When I said we're together, I just took it for granted.

'I know we haven't known each other for very long but you've been so good to me and we do get on very well. Wouldn't you like us to see how it progresses? I mean, will you be my girlfriend?'

'That sounds a bit quaint but yes, of course I will. I'd love to be your girlfriend and to see where it'll take us.'

Olly held out his hands and she went to him. Gently, he put his arms round her and kissed her tenderly. She snuggled against him.

'Ouch!' he said suddenly.

'Oh, my goodness. I'm so sorry,' she said.

'Just a bit painful round the ribs.' He smiled apologetically.

'I completely forgot. Couldn't even see your damaged face with my eyes closed.'

'That sounds good to me. Tomorrow, We'll go back to my house and make a start on the rest of our lives. What do you think?'

'I think that sounds so good.'

★ ★ ★

Later, as she lay in bed, Sarah-Louise smiled to herself. This business with Jeannie was a purely temporary affair, she felt certain. Their friendship would soon be back on track.

Her own future with Olly seemed secure. Even if she had only known him for a short while, she felt sure this was going to be the real thing.

The future looked so good.